SLATE

Nathan Aldyne

Villard Books   New York   1984

For Paul Church

Library of Congress Cataloging in Publication Data

Aldyne, Nathan.
  Slate.

    I. Title.
PS3551.L346S55   1984   813'.54   83-21892
ISBN 0-394-53697-5

Manufactured in the United States of America

9 8 7 6 5 4 3 2

First Edition

Part One

Chapter One

CLARISSE LOVELACE stumbled into the main lobby of Beth Israel Hospital. Struggling to balance three bunches of flowers, a two-pound Whitman's Sampler, four paperback books, and a briefcase, she tripped over the threshold and slipped a contact lens. She staggered over to the information desk, squinted at the clock above the bank of cathode-ray tubes bristling with hospital information, and was relieved to find that half an hour of morning visiting hours remained.

Blinking violently in hope that the errant lens would slip back into place, she made her way to the elevators and deftly punched the up button with her elbow. In a moment, the green signal flashed with a resounding bong and the doors opened. She smiled to see the elevator empty and then stepped inside.

Before she could angle her elbow around to punch the button for the fourth floor, however, seven persons in the lobby caught sight of the open doors and rushed inside. Clarisse was pressed against the side wall; the box of candy, the flowers, and the books were crushed against her breasts. Because she was nearest the control panel, her fellow passengers barked demands that she press buttons for their floors. A large, determined-looking woman with a shopping bag swinging in the crook of her arm charged toward the elevator shouting, "Going up! Going up!" Frantically Clarisse stabbed her elbow against the disk marked Door Close. The chrome doors slid smoothly shut, and the woman's curses followed them upward.

"I said two, lady!" snapped a man in the corner, as the elevator slipped past the second floor.

"Hey, I got to—" began another man, nearer Clarisse, but still out of reach of the panel. "If my brother dies before I get to see him, it'll be your fault!" he concluded acidly as the elevator rose past three.

"Did you push seven?" demanded a women who was completely invisible to Clarisse. "Chemotherapy's on seven."

When the doors opened at four, Clarisse pressed her arm against the panel so that buttons for all the floors were lighted. "Everybody satisfied?" she asked politely, and struggled out. In doing so, she lost one of her three bouquets—the one of white asters. A little boy in the front of the crowd jumped up and down on the flowers and then kicked them out into the corridor after Clarisse.

Glaring murderously at the child, Clarisse dropped everything she was carrying, picked up the smashed bouquet and flung it into the elevator. The passengers were showered with petals, wet stems, and bits of green paper. Their outrage was cut short by the closing doors.

"Clarisse?" inquired a female voice curiously, as Clarisse knelt to retrieve her gifts.

She stood up and smiled uncertainly at a young nurse with a tumble of red hair. Her name tag read *K. Reardon*. The nurse smiled, and adjusted the books in Clarisse's arms for better balance.

Clarisse looked at her for a few moments, and then said authoritatively, "Appleton Street duplex. Garden and roof deck.

Eight-fifty a month, plus utilities." Then she apologized: "I'm sorry, I remember your apartment, but not your first name."

"Katherine," said the nurse. "I haven't seen you around the office lately when I've gone to pay the rent." The office was South End Realty where Clarisse had worked as an agent for several years.

"I spent the summer in P'town," explained Clarisse. "And I've given up real estate. I'm starting law school—tomorrow, as a matter of fact. Portia School of Law, on Beacon Hill."

"That's great," said the nurse. "Criminal?"

"No, I think I'm going corporate."

Katherine nodded approval and then, indicating the gifts, asked, "Who are you seeing?"

Clarisse told her the room number.

"Oh," said Katherine Reardon, her smile draining away with dark implications. "The doll by the window or the martyr by the door?"

"Daniel Valentine," replied Clarisse.

"The martyr." The nurse sighed with sympathy. "I don't know if candy and flowers and books are going to be enough. I think that one's a job for Mother Theresa."

———

———

"WELL," said Clarisse, turning around before Valentine at the foot of the bed, "how do you like the new me?" She wore a tailored gray suit and a white blouse. Her hose were a darker shade of gray than the suit; her high heels, belt, and tie were black. Vermilion lipstick, emphasizing her full mouth, was in startling contrast.

She had placed her briefcase at the foot of the bed and arranged the gifts on top of the metal table beside the door of the double room. She made a perfunctory and unsuccessful attempt to glance around the curtain that separated Valentine from his roommate. The roommate was talking volubly on the telephone, but unfortunately for Valentine and Clarisse's curiosity, in a low, unintelligible voice.

"Well?" she prompted, turning again.

Valentine didn't answer. A clear plastic oxygen mask covered his mouth and nose. An intravenous tube led from a needle buried in his left forearm up to a bottle of clear liquid suspended from a portable hanger. His eyes were heavy lidded and dull; his summer tan had almost faded, and his short blond hair and neatly trimmed beard had grown darker. The pneumonia that had put Valentine in the hospital had debilitated his body for the past eight weeks, but had only been diagnosed ten days before. He had entered the hospital the day after he was laid off from his job as a social worker at the Charles Street Jail. Daniel Valentine looked just about as bad as he felt.

"Well?" Clarisse repeated. "I'm not going to leave until I get a reply."

"*Mmmmgggffffsssnnnnnn*," said Valentine.

"What?" Clarisse asked. Leaning over, she pried up the oxygen mask.

"You look magnificent," he answered in a husky, labored voice.

She smiled and withdrew her fingers. The mask snapped back into place. Valentine winced.

"Registration at Portia is this afternoon. I thought I might as well start out right, so Raymond cut my hair this morning. Don't you think it looks great?" Her black hair, previously worn in flowing waves or in intricate chignons, was now cut in a straightforward, fashionable style that brushed her shoulders. "Don't you think it says about me—vaguely, I mean—*This woman will make a great corporate lawyer. This woman is worth any amount of money at all in retainer fees. This woman will never lose a case in the entire span of her lengthy and brilliant career?*" She turned and glanced in the mirror. "That's what *I* think it says." She turned back to Valentine. "And a new wardrobe—I got a new wardrobe. So far it has cost me more than the first year's tuition, and I haven't even *looked* at shoes yet. This is my power look," she concluded with a ravishing smile. "The problem is that the power look has thrust me very deeply into poverty."

Valentine rolled his eyes.

"Don't you want to know what I brought you?" she asked. He nodded. "Flowers," she said, holding up the bouquets and waving them beneath his mask. "Whitman's Sampler—your favorite." She pulled the ribbon off the box of candy and slit the plastic wrap with a sharp fingernail. "Some books—light reading for those hours that hang so heavy." She held up the covers for him to see. Three were novels—one by Cornell Woolrich, one by James M. Cain, and one by Marion Zimmer Bradley—and the fourth was Lana Turner's autobiography. Valentine's eyes widened, and he pointed excitedly to the Lana Turner book. Clarisse handed it to him, and with strength provided by an adrenaline rush he heaved it over her shoulder so that it slammed against the far wall and slid neatly down into the trash can in the corner.

"I guess you've read it already," said Clarisse. "Well, let me put these flowers in some water, and then we have to talk a little business."

She took up the bouquets, then grabbed a couple of urine specimen bottles from Valentine's bedside table and started for the bathroom.

At that moment a hand came around the curtain dividing the room, clutched the material, and pulled it back. The hoops clattered along the rod. Clarisse prepared a smile for "the doll by the window," as Katherine Reardon had called Valentine's roommate.

Despite that description, Clarisse was mildly startled by how markedly handsome the man was. His curly hair was a couple of shades darker than Valentine's, but still could be called blond. He had strong, clean-shaven features, a ruddy complexion, and pale blue eyes. His green johnny was open to the waist and his smooth chest was plaited with defined muscle. His mouth was turned up in a half-smile as he studied Clarisse.

"I wanted to see the power look," he said.

"You don't think it's too much?" Clarisse asked him without hesitation.

"I think you look just fine. Like Glenda Jackson when she's had enough sleep. My name's Linc. Lincoln, really, but everybody calls me Linc."

"I'm Clarisse. I'm visiting Valentine." She pushed the curtain all the way back to the wall. Valentine made a noise behind his mask as he busily discarded the peanut clusters from the Whitman's Sampler. "You haven't met?" Clarisse asked Linc.

"I was brought in late last night," he explained. "Your friend was asleep."

"Linc," said Clarisse, "this is Daniel Valentine. Val, this is Linc . . ."

"Hamilton," said the man, and waved to Valentine in lieu of a handshake. Valentine set the candy aside, waved back, and then collapsed against his pillows in apparent exhaustion.

"What's he in for?" Linc asked.

"Double walking pneumonia. He carried it around for almost two months."

Linc looked puzzled.

"What is it?" asked Clarisse.

"I thought he was in for a nervous breakdown."

"What?"

"That's what Sweeney Drysdale II said in his column in the *BAR*."

"The bar?" echoed Clarisse vaguely. "Is that a new place?"

"No, it's a paper. The *Boston Area Reporter*. It's a free rag they give out in all the bars. It's down there in that pile of papers," said Linc, pointing at a small stack of newspapers beneath his nightstand. "Hand them to me and I'll find it."

"And this man," said Clarisse slowly, leaning over and gathering up the papers, "said that Valentine had had a nervous breakdown, and that was why he was in the hospital?"

"Right," returned Linc.

Clarisse paused pensively. "Maybe we'll sue. Maybe *I'll* sue. Maybe it could be my first case." She turned back to Linc. "Do lots of people read this paper?"

"Sure," said Linc, picking through the newspapers. "Everybody does, 'cause they're free. There's *BAR*, and *Jason's Thing*, and there's a third one, but it's no good because all the articles in it are about Syracuse. Nobody reads that one." He found the *BAR* and held it up for Clarisse to see the front page. Then, as he opened it and began leafing through, he continued: "These papers give the bar news, and listings, and somebody writes an article about how he got to shake hands with the man who's playing Daddy Warbucks at the Chateau de Ville Dinner Theatre, and some leather man writes a concerned letter to the community about how retarded children don't have enough toys. There's always a gossip column and they talk about bartenders and their friends, except nobody really knows who they are. Here it is."

He folded the tabloid-size paper and handed it to Clarisse, pointing out the column. "I remembered your friend because his name was Valentine. I used to think they made all that gossip up, you know, because nobody I knew had ever even *heard* of these people. And all the gossip columnists have fights and say nasty things about one another. Of course, three-fourths of the magazines are just ads. That's why they print them, for the ads."

Clarisse had found the item she had been searching for, and impatiently riding over the last of Linc's speech, she read aloud: ". . . *Following a hot P'town summer of surf, sand, and sin, Daniel Valentine and his friend Clarisse Lovelace have returned to Boston. Unfortunately for the buzzing barflies of Beantown, Mr. Valentine is temporarily out of circulation, but may be found holding court in Beth Israel Hospital. Clarisse says he has only a little cold—'no more than a sniffle, really' — but others whisper it may be 'no more than a little nervous breakdown. Really!' over the loss of his job counseling prisoners in the Charles Street Jail, thanks to the most recent round of city budget slashings . . ."* Clarisse looked at Linc. "I'm going to look into this," she said. "You just can't go around saying that somebody has had a nervous breakdown. Valentine," she remarked casually over her shoulder, "how'd you like to be party to a multimillion-dollar libel suit?"

Clarisse was showered with a handful of candy wrappers.

"And they quote me, too," she mused. "I certainly don't recall being hounded by reporters in the past few weeks." She turned back to Linc. "You look healthy enough," she said suddenly. "What's wrong with you?"

"A low-grade infection. I'm only going to be here for a couple of days, so don't waste too much sympathy."

"I promise," said Clarisse. "What I want to know is, will you do me a favor?"

"Probably," Linc responded immediately. "Anything within the law — and some things out of it."

"Not much," said Clarisse. "Just keep an eye on this one." She glanced in Valentine's direction. "He's not supposed to sit up, talk on the telephone, or do anything except a long-term imitation of a winter vegetable. If he tries anything, just jump up and down on top of his lungs, and that'll put a crimp in his style."

"Be glad to," said Linc.

At that moment Linc's telephone rang again and he said, "Excuse me." He picked up the receiver and, with a polite smile of apology, pulled the curtain shut again.

Clarisse suddenly realized that she was still holding the specimen bottles. She went into the bathroom, filled the bottles with water, and arranged her tea roses and black-eyed Susans in them. She walked back out into the room and placed the bottles on the table at the side of Valentine's bed. He put aside the current issue of *The Journal of the American Playing Card Association* as she pulled a chair up close and sat down. Beyond the curtain they could hear Linc telling one of his friends, in considerable detail, the plot of the fifty-fifth volume of *The Destroyer* series.

"Now to business," Clarisse said in a low voice. "And try to forget, for a few moments, that the Hunk of Death is lying in bed just on the other side of that curtain." Crossing her legs, she took a pack of cigarettes and a book of matches from her jacket.

Valentine's eyes widened. One hand flew up wildly—nearly dislodging the needle in his vein—and pointed to the oxygen system built into the wall. Beside it was a placard fully one foot square, reading ABSOLUTELY NO SMOKING. He simulated the sound of an explosion behind his mask. With a grimace, Clarisse put away the cigarettes, but she kept the book of matches and played with them nervously.

"All right now," she said, glancing at her watch, "I have just ten minutes left of visiting time, and in that ten minutes I'm going to put your whole life back in order."

Valentine mumbled beneath his mask.

"So what if you've got double pneumonia?" shrugged Clarisse. "So what if you lost your job? So what if you don't have the money for next month's rent? We're both in our thirties now, and I've decided that it's time our lives were going somewhere."

Feigning terminal exhaustion, he motioned for her to lift his mask.

"Bonaparte's," he whispered.

She dropped the mask derisively. "Bartending will not make you rich. Bartending will not make your name familiar in the circles of power and fashion. It's time to move on. Besides, you don't want to go back to that place anyway. You hate the new manager and he hates you. I know this is all very sudden, but you're not going to have to go back. I've fixed everything."

Valentine raised his right eyebrow.

"Noah's been in town for the last few days," said Clarisse airily, referring to her uncle. "He's closed up the restaurant in P'town, and tomorrow he's on his way to Morocco for the winter. Did you know that he owns those two buildings across from the District D police station in the South End?"

Valentine shook his head and mumbled.

"Sam's Bar and Grill—where I used to go for lunch every day. Best grease in town. Mr. Fred's Tease 'n' Tint is next door. And apartments upstairs."

Valentine shrugged.

"Well," said Clarisse quickly, "Sam—except his name wasn't really Sam—is retiring and getting out. As of next Monday Sam's Bar and Grill is no more. Except, of course, the liquor license stays. So Noah's got a bar and he's got a license that's probably worth a hundred thousand dollars, and he wants to know if you want to open up a place of your own. That is, he'll finance it and you'll set everything up—arrange for renovations, the other licenses, hiring, publicity, and all. Then you'll manage it and get half the profits for the first two years. Then, depending upon how things go, you and Noah can renegotiate terms." Clarisse paused and took a long breath.

Valentine was sitting up straight now. Clarisse reached over and gently pressed him down in the bed again.

"Interested?" she asked. "I thought so. It needs a lot of work, though. Sam's never did have the kind of decor to attract clones—or anybody else, for that matter. The other thing is, the three apartments above the bar are ours, if we want them."

Valentine wrinkled his brow.

"Ours *free*," she went on. "I'm going to take the two-bedroom. Life is hard when you're an ambitious, dedicated student of corporate law, and I've decided that a rent-free two-bedroom flat in an up-and-coming neighborhood is just the sort of thing to keep up my spirits during my first semester. You can have the one-bedroom. It's a little smaller than the place you've got now, but you're going to be so busy setting up the bar that you're not even going to notice. And the good thing is we can move in immediately—or as soon as I evict the gypsies."

Valentine groaned.

"Are you interested?"

Valentine nodded.

"Very interested?"

He nodded again.

"Are you willing to sign papers?"

He hesitated.

"As I said, Noah is leaving for Morocco tomorrow, so everything *has* to be done tonight. I've already typed up the forms and I know a notary public who'll make a hospital call and so forth. Listen, there's really nothing to worry about. You're only signing away your life. No matter what happens in the end, you won't be any worse off than you are at this very moment."

He glanced at her skeptically and slowly lifted the mask. "I'll sign," he murmured huskily, "on one condition."

"What?"

He gasped for the oxygen. "That you"—he gasped again—"give up smoking."

Clarisse, overtaken with horror, allowed the mask to snap smartly back. Valentine, breathing stertorously, fell back against the pillow.

"You're serious, aren't you?" she said, aghast. "Give up cigarettes?" she whispered.

"I'll be tempted every time I see you light up," said Valentine gravely. "Besides, I won't be able to do it unless I know you're suffering, too."

Clarisse stood up, thrust her shoulders back, dropped the book of matches to the floor, and ground it beneath her heel. She took the pack of cigarettes from her jacket, held it in both hands and twisted it until the cellophane wrapping split and loose tobacco sprinkled out of the open end onto the sheet over Valentine's legs. She went over to the trash can and ripped the pack apart, showering paper, cellophane, foil, and tobacco over Lana Turner. She took a deep breath and turned back to Valentine. "I swear, Valentine, not one more milligram of tar will smudge my lungs. I will be as healthy as the day is long. Come to think of it, I don't think I could smoke in court anyway."

Linc, finished with his telephone call at last, pulled back the curtain once again.

"Linc," said Clarisse, turning toward him, "entertain this man until I return."

"I will," he promised.

"I'll be back this evening, Val," said Clarisse, her shoulders still thrown stiffly back, with the air of a moral martyr, "with Noah, a notary, and five thousand pieces of paper for you to sign. This is the beginning of a whole new existence for us—new careers, new styles of life, and new health for our poor abused lungs."

"Goodbye," said Linc. "It was nice meeting you."

Clarisse went to the head of Valentine's bed, touched his cheek with her knuckles, and turned bravely away. Taking up her briefcase, she rushed from the room, ran down the corridor, and slipped between the closing doors of the elevator. Downstairs, she flew across the lobby and stiff-armed her way through the revolving door. Outside, she tripped on the curb and nearly fell under the wheels of the taxi she had flagged. Flinging herself into the back seat, she slammed the door shut and exclaimed breathlessly, "Take me to the nearest cigarette machine!"

Chapter Two

BAY VILLAGE was characteristically quiet on the crisp Saturday morning in October when Clarisse turned wearily onto Fayette Street. Valentine's neighborhood was alarmingly picturesque: small mid-Victorian row houses exquisitely maintained, clean narrow streets, and baroque music from a first-floor flat the only sound. The sun was bright in a cloudless sky. Just out of sight of Valentine's building, Clarisse yawned and dropped her cigarette onto the brick sidewalk. She crushed it out beneath the heel of her riding boot and flicked it into the gutter with the toe.

Valentine's lungs had cleared after eleven days in the hospital, and he had apparently remained firm in his decision never to smoke again. For one thing, he wouldn't be able to afford to, considering the size of his medical bill. Clarisse, without the impetus of double walking pneumonia, was having difficulty maintaining her promise to him. When they were together, she often sneaked smokes in restaurant restrooms or leaning out of his kitchen window. She grimly noted that she never really enjoyed these cigarettes or smoked more than half of them. And Valentine often complained of the heavy, nauseating lavender odor from the air freshener that hung in her apartment.

She now popped a green breath mint into her mouth and paused for a moment until it began to melt on her tongue. She nodded a sleepy smile to an elderly man walking a snarling Doberman.

When she entered the narrow foyer of Valentine's building she regarded her reflection in the glass of the inside doors and groaned. She looked as if she hadn't slept or changed clothes in twenty-four hours. In fact, this was the case. She straightened the coral sweater beneath her waist-length leather jacket and pressed her thumb against Daniel's buzzer.

"Yes?" Valentine's voice came immediately and with a cheery tinniness through the small speaker in the middle of the four mailboxes. It was early in the morning, and she had so very much expected a long delay in his answering that she was at a loss to say anything.

"Who is it?" Valentine repeated patiently.

"A victim of caffeine withdrawal," Clarisse croaked at last.

"Madam," said Valentine, "this is not a drug crisis center." A moment later the inner door buzzed, automatically releasing the catch. As Clarisse pushed through the heavy oak door her eyes fell upon a single work boot lying in the corner of the foyer. It was much scuffed, but the thick red laces were new. Glancing around the hallway, but not finding its mate, she placed the boot neatly atop an advertising circular on the small deal table beneath the entrance hall mirror. On her way up to the second floor she noticed a number of coins of various denominations scattered over the carpeted stairs.

On the second landing, Valentine's apartment door was open for her. She went inside. Sitting on the edge of the sofa was a man wearing a yellow construction hat, a loosely fitting brown-plaid flannel shirt over a long-sleeved red T-shirt, and faded blue jeans that snugly defined his muscular legs. One foot was encased in a work boot with red laces, and the other showed only his thick gray woolen sock.

He looked up at her and smiled. "Hello, Clarisse."

"Your other boot is downstairs," she returned with her own smile, though she hadn't the least idea in the world who the man might be. "I put it on the table."

"Thanks," he said. "Thought I might have left it in the taxi."

"And your subway fare is scattered on the stairs," she added, looking with curiosity down the narrow hall to the back of the apartment. "That *was* Valentine who buzzed me in, wasn't it?"

"Be out in a second," Valentine called from the bedroom.

The construction worker stood up, a little off-balance in only one boot. "Tell him I've gone to the market for juice. Does he like orange or grapefruit?"

"Orange," answered Clarisse. She stepped aside as the man stepped past her with a sheepish grin and went to gather up his coins on the way down the stairs. Below, she heard him as he struggled into his boot and then threw himself with a crash out the door.

Barefoot, Valentine appeared in the hall, threading a leather belt through the loops of his jeans.

"Who was that?" demanded Clarisse, stabbing a thumb toward the hallway. "He knew who I was."

"Lincoln Hamilton," said Valentine. He motioned her to follow him into the kitchen.

"Good Lord," breathed Clarisse after a moment's reflection. "That was the man next to you in the hospital? I didn't recognize him at all. Is the construction drag real?"

Valentine nodded with satisfaction. "You want a cup of coffee, I assume." He took three mugs from the cupboard.

"Just give it to me in a hypodermic," said Clarisse, sitting at the table by the window. "The caffeine will work faster that way. Did you two make this date in the hospital?"

"No, I ran into him last night over at Chaps. I went there because I knew I'd come home alone. Attitude City. When somebody gets picked up at Chaps, the DJ stops the music, a woman in a red velvet harness swings down from the ceiling, the bartenders pass out cigars, and the bouncer pounds a star into the floor. Anyway, Linc was there, and the rest you probably don't want to hear about in any kind of detail."

"I certainly don't," said Clarisse peevishly. "Valentine, I want you to know that while you were here doing whatever it was that you two were doing all night long, I suffered through a night of living hell. I was psychologically abused, placed in mortal physical danger, and cursed in an obscure foreign tongue."

"You had another date with that Swedish architect?"

"No," said Clarisse balefully. "I spent the evening evicting the gypsies. I'll tell you something, Daniel Valentine: I am very angry with my uncle."

"What did Noah do?"

"Well, if you remember—while you and he were having a fine old time signing agreement papers in the hospital, he casually mentioned that I would have the pleasant task of persuading an entire tribe of squatters to vacate the building they've called home for the past five years."

"I remember, vaguely. Maybe he should have done something about those people before now."

"Noah didn't care! It was just a tax write-off for him. One of those upper-bracket dodges that nobody but a tax accountant really understands."

The door buzzer sounded, and Valentine went into the front room to buzz Linc inside. A few moments later they both came back into the kitchen. Linc had bought not only orange juice but Danishes.

Clarisse nodded pleasantly to Linc and then continued talking to Valentine. "Somehow Noah made more money *not* collecting rent from them than he would have if they had paid on the first of the month." Clarisse sighed. "I guess I shouldn't complain about what I had to do—after all, he's giving us the place free."

"Is this the bar you want to open?" Linc asked, leaning back and stretching out his legs. He pushed his construction hat back on his head.

"I told Linc about your railroading me into this," Valentine said to Clarisse. He took a bite of Danish. "When do we get to move in?" He looked around him doubtfully, as if unsure he was ready to give up his present apartment.

"Not quite yet," said Clarisse vaguely. "The former tenants left a bit of a mess. It may take a little while to get things in shape."

"How many people were living there?" asked Linc.

"Seven adults, nine children. Of course that was just the top-floor apartment."

"You threw sixteen people out onto the street?" Valentine exclaimed.

"Well," Clarisse conceded, "maybe not that many, but they were moving so fast that I probably kept counting them over and over. But don't waste your time feeling sorry for them—remember how long they'd been there without paying rent. Not to mention that half the neighborhood was out there cheering me on. These were not people who made a lot of friends during their freeloading tenure."

"You make it sound like you routed the PLO. Exactly how did you perform this eviction?"

"Don't make me relive it, please," groaned Clarisse, slugging down the last of her coffee. "Maybe someday I'll be well enough to tell you about it." She staggered to her feet and wandered toward the coffeepot again.

Linc nudged Valentine's bare foot with the steel toe of his boot. "You want to show me around your new bar?"

"Sure," said Valentine.

"Now?" said Clarisse. "Couldn't you make it later? Like next month or something? I thought I'd spend a pleasant Saturday morning hiding between sheets. I tried to make it home this morning, but my feet started sending out distress signals."

"I'm a carpenter," Linc explained to her. "I love to see unrenovated buildings. I think it helps to sharpen my technique."

"As far as I'm concerned," said Valentine, "your technique is just fine."

"Maybe I can give you some ideas," said Linc. "About the renovations, I mean."

"How much do you know about modern demolition techniques?" Clarisse asked and drained half the mug of coffee.

———

———

TWENTY minutes later, Clarisse, Valentine, and Linc Hamilton stood in front of the District D police station, staring across Warren Avenue at the two buildings owned by Clarisse's uncle, Noah Lovelace. Warren Avenue was typical of many streets in Boston's South End, where restored elegance stood in direct, jarring contrast to decaying ruins. Those who lived there claimed this contrast was part of the area's charm; others longed for the hour when gentrification would be complete. The trio stood on the sidewalk in front of the large brick and stone station house. Policemen went in and out with spasmodic regularity. Once a docile but handcuffed prisoner was wrenched out of the back seat of a squad car and hustled up the short flight of steps into the building.

The two buildings owned by Noah Lovelace, and now in Valentine's care, were the sole structures on one end of a narrow triangular block formed by Warren Avenue, Tremont Street, and Clarendon Street. Not too many years before the houses on either side had been torn down. Beyond the vacant lot on one side was the gray stone back of the Boston Center for the Arts, extending all the way up to Clarendon Street. On the other side, a small, abandoned playground was littered with beer cans, liquor and wine bottles, smashed hypodermic syringes, cans of Lysol and Sterno, cigarette butts, and stained sanitary napkins.

The two buildings were four-story town houses, whose

ground floors had long before been given over to commercial ventures. A weathered metal sign for Sam's Bar and Grill swayed gently above the shadowed recess of the wide doorway to the bar. The windows on either side of it had been painted black. A narrow doorway to the right of this opened onto a stairwell leading to the apartments on the upper floors.

The storefront of the adjacent building was occupied by Mr. Fred's Tease 'n' Tint. Its large plate-glass window was dark. Behind it there was a suggestion of purple and lime-green decor.

"I wouldn't think he had much off-the-street trade," said Linc, looking doubtfully at a large border of sun-faded Agfacolor photographs, circa 1963, of women modeling "exotic hairdos."

"You'd be surprised," said Clarisse. "At any rate, the street is where most of his customers have their trade."

"Oh," said Linc. "I see."

"You know," said Valentine at last, "this city doesn't really need another gay bar."

"Ummm . . ." Linc agreed.

"No," Clarisse granted, "it certainly doesn't need just *another* one, but it sure could stand a really *good* one—the kind of bar you'd like to go to yourself."

"How do we know Boston *wants* a good bar? I could be back on the unemployment line by Christmas. Except this time I'd be neck-deep in debt."

"When was the last time you ever heard of anybody with a liquor license going bankrupt?" Linc asked.

"That's right. You could make money out of a Dempsey Dumpster if it had a liquor license," Clarisse added.

They crossed the street. The line of police cars had obscured their vision of the sidewalk in front of the bar. Perplexed, Valentine stopped short. In front of the bar was a scattering of broken pottery, a smashed television set angled into the gutter, and a pile of heavily soiled and torn garments wrapped high around the pole of a parking meter. Two large boxes of food lay split open and spilled in the recess of the doorway. Everywhere there was broken glass.

"What the hell happened here?" asked Valentine.

"*This*," said Clarisse meaningfully, "was the battlefield." She pushed through the wreckage to the door of Sam's Bar and Grill, then took a large ring of keys from her pocket and began trying one after another. "I meant to mark which of these was which," she grumbled.

Linc looked up at the facade of the building. Some of the broken glass had evidently come from windows smashed out above. Dirty red curtains billowed through the broken panes.

"I thought you said you got everybody out," he remarked.

"I did."

"Well, there's somebody upstairs. I just saw them step back from the window."

"Me too," Valentine said.

"Third or fourth floor?"

"Third," Valentine and Linc answered.

"Oh, that's all right. That's Julia Logan and Susie Whitebread. They have the third-floor front. You'll be neighbors."

"*Whitebread?*" Valentine repeated incredulously. "How cute can you get?"

"Well, I don't actually think it's her real name," Clarisse admitted. "But it's how she signed her lease."

Valentine eyed her warily. "I want to know more about this one."

Clarisse shrugged. "She claims she was a slave in a former existence and that Whitebread was the name her cruel master gave her."

Valentine groaned. "What you mean is, is that she's a white woman with a black fetish. And I'll bet she talks like she just walked in from the cotton fields, right?"

"Something like that . . ."

"Is the other one black? Julia?"

"Yes," said Clarisse uncomfortably.

"I'm moving in next door to a walking cliché."

"They always pay their rent on time," said Clarisse. "Julia repairs swimming pools for a living. She gets flown all over the country at a moment's notice. She's the best in her field."

"And Miss Whitebread? What does she do now that cotton-picking season is over?"

Clarisse took a deep breath, and said quickly, "Susie dates a lot."

Linc's eyebrows rose questioningly, and Valentine kicked idly at a box of food. Powdery meal from an open package shot up in a little dun-colored plume. "I refuse to live across the hall from a hooker," Valentine said in a low voice. "They're noisy and bad for security. They answer the buzzer for anybody."

"Susie is not a *hooker*," said Clarisse in a hot whisper, rattling the keys. "She's a *call girl*—an *out*-call girl. And besides, she's recording secretary for PUMA."

"What's that?"

"The Prostitutes Union of Massachusetts," Linc cut in.

"And if that's not respectability, I don't know what is," said Clarisse. "She's certainly the only call girl I ever met who had a résumé. She and Julia are very respectable, very responsible, and very much in love. They're so quiet you'll think you're living across the hall from two librarians with narcolepsy. Besides, Noah already told them they could stay."

Clarisse took out a second ring of keys from her jacket pocket. Valentine and Linc wandered over to the window of Mr. Fred's and intently examined the photographs of beehives and bubble cuts.

After a few moments they went back to Clarisse, who was still struggling with keys.

"What's this Mr. Fred like?" Valentine asked.

"He saved my life last night," said Clarisse offhandedly.

"Really?" Linc asked, impressed. "How?"

"Well, when the two teenaged girls threw the television set off the fire escape at me, he yelled *'Jump'*."

Both Valentine and Linc looked at the smashed set in the gutter.

"They threw *that* off the fire escape at you?" Valentine asked, glancing up.

"See what I mean?" said Clarisse, at last pressing the correct key into the lock. "Mr. Fred saved my life."

She grasped the two large handles and yanked the heavy doors outward. The hinges squealed metallically. Sunlight glinted briefly off two round windows in the inner red-leather padded doors as Clarisse and Valentine pushed them open, bracing for the first glimpse of their new life.

Chapter Three

THE LINOLEUM on the floor of the barroom had been patched in so many places that the original pattern was entirely lost. From the cracked red vinyl on the battered barstools, to the dingy forty-eight-star American flags that were stapled to the wall above the mirrored bar, the building stank of grease, cigarettes, and old alchohol.

The room itself was two stories high. A scarred mahogany bar ran along the right side; three booths and four tables had been installed haphazardly along the left wall. Battered wainscoting lined the walls to a height of about six feet. Above it, cheap composition board paneling reached to the ceiling.

Valentine leaned against a shelf that had been bolted between two iron pillars, and looked around dismally.

Clarisse, with an eager gesture, pointed upward. "See, fan-and-globe lights. You know how much you love fan-and-globe lights. And just look at that ceiling!"

"You mean the fact that it's about two feet lower at the front than at the back? Or the fact that it's been completely discolored with thirty years of smoke and grease?"

"It's a wonderful ceiling," Clarisse insisted. "Tin. And the pattern is squares with borders of shamrocks. Perfect for St. Patrick's Day."

Valentine pushed himself away from the shelf, and went behind the bar. The mirrors there badly needed resilvering, and the shelving for liquor bottles was glazed with years of dust and grime. In back of the bar, a swinging door with a diamond of glass led into what Clarisse said was the kitchen. An ice machine sat in a fair-sized puddle of filthy water against the wall in the back of the barroom. Toward the left of that, now open and exposing a rectangle of black, was a trapdoor with an iron ring handle. Below, Clarisse told them, was a storage cellar for liquors, wines, and other supplies.

To the right of the front door was an ugly, floor-to-ceiling boxy construction with a narrow doorway. A mirror facing the bar was set into the upper portion of the structure. Clarisse eagerly explained that the top section was a small office—all that remained of the original second floor of the building. The mirror was a one-way glass. A short spiral staircase connected the office to the floor level and, Clarisse continued, the interior of the lower area would make an ideal coat check.

Valentine looked at everything in sullen silence. Linc, however, regarded all the things that depressed Valentine merely as potential for a clever and thorough renovation.

Clarisse wandered over to the wall of booths. She tugged at a loose piece of the thin, cheap paneling. "This stuff has definitely got to go."

"Why don't we just pump the whole damn place full of ammonia for about two months and then come look at it again?" Valentine said with a labored sigh, poking his head into the potentially ideal coat check.

"You're just crabby because you gave up smoking. If you had a cigarette right now, this place wouldn't seem so bad. I realize it isn't exactly what you were expecting . . ."

"Actually," he said, stepping back, "it's a bit more than I expected."

"Well," said Linc brightly, coming from behind the bar, "I'd like to see the rest of the place."

Clarisse led them through the coat check and up the rickety spiral staircase. At the top she scraped open a low door and turned on a dim overhead light in the office.

The room was no more than twelve feet by ten. A wooden chair lay on its side on the dusty floor and a small table with two legs was clumsily nailed to one of the walls. A pinup calendar from 1967 was thumbtacked above it. Linc glanced out the one-way mirror, but it was so grimy he could scarcely make out the murky glow of the fan-and-globe lights.

Valentine looked about, frowned, and shook his head. "This is getting more discouraging by the minute, Lovelace."

"Too late for cold feet," she replied briskly. "Now come on, I'll show you your new apartment."

A second door in the office gave entrance to the private part of the building. From a tiny dark landing, a narrow staircase descended to a street door. More stairs rose to the two apartments on the third floor, and the larger apartment on the fourth.

Leading the two men up to the narrow third-floor hallway, Clarisse unlocked a door painted Chinese red with forest-green insert panels. From behind a door across the hall came the muted noise of a cheering crowd.

"Sounds like business is booming for the resident call girl," Valentine said.

"That's just the television," said Clarisse. "Susie and Julia have the last three years of *Wide World of Sports* on tape. 'Demolition Derby' is their favorite, though."

She reached inside the door and snapped on a garish light. Inside, the walls of the empty living room were painted a pink so hot it seemed to vibrate in its intensity. The woodwork and the window sashes were painted two shades of blue.

"Your new abode," Clarisse said cheerfully.

Linc drew a sharp breath and let it out slowly.

"Oh, God," Valentine groaned. He walked across the room and pulled open a set of slatted folding doors, revealing a tiny kitchen, with lemon-yellow walls and all the appliances that same color. Valentine slammed shut the folding doors, and turned to Clarisse, whose eyes were averted. "What color is the bedroom?" he demanded.

Linc peeked into a room directly across from the kitchen. "Crimson," he said in a low voice.

"There's still a bed in there," Clarisse said. "But I don't know if I'd call it the kind of bed you'd want to lie down on. The sheets got up and shook my hand."

Valentine grimaced. He made no move toward the bedroom. "I've seen enough for today. While the bar is filled with ammonia, we can shoot this place full of turpentine. Christ, Lovelace, look at this apartment—Whore's Haven. It'll take weeks just to strip the baseboards and the floors, and it'll take three coats of paint to bury these colors."

"At least," Linc agreed.

"Whoa, child!" exclaimed a loud voice behind them. "You could get third-degree burns just walkin' *through* this place."

Valentine, Clarisse, and Linc turned. Clarisse smiled automatically at the woman leaning against the doorframe. She was slender and pretty, with a fair complexion, large eyes, and sharp features. Her dyed black hair was permed into soft ringlets. The one-piece blouse-and-shorts outfit was soft blue and too tight, clearly outlining the sleek curves of her slim, athletic body. Her long legs were encased in black hose, and her feet were strapped into high cork-heel wedgies. She dangled an opened can of Busch beer from the long fingers of her right hand.

"Susie," said Clarisse, "this is Daniel Valentine and Linc Hamilton. Daniel will be your new neighbor. He'll be running the bar downstairs."

Susie offered her hand from the door. She didn't seem inclined to come farther inside. Valentine stepped forward and shook it.

"The proper word, by the way, is *prostitute*," she said with a smile. "Not *whore*, not even *hooker*."

"I'm sorry," said Valentine sincerely. "I honestly am."

"It's okay." Susie shrugged. "But I am an officer—of PUMA, you know? And I wouldn't be doing my sworn duty if I didn't stand up for the semantics clause in our constitution." She glanced over the apartment once more and shook her head. "Lordy, these walls could give sight to the blind." She took a long sip of her beer.

"At least you've got a view," said Linc, gazing out the window.

Susie looked about again, and again shook her head. "You all come next door and I'll give everybody a beer and cold compresses for your eyes."

Susie and Julia's apartment was the same layout as Valentine's, except that its windows looked out onto Warren Avenue and the police station. The furnishings were a mixture of decent pieces from the forties and early fifties. Angled into one corner was an enormous color television set linked to stereo speakers and a video recorder. Set into another corner was a small desk with a black push-button telephone, an answering machine, and a thick address book opened next to it.

When Susie went into the kitchen, Valentine went immediately to the desk and glanced at the address book. He turned to Clarisse, and hissed, "It's all in code." Clarisse shot a look of disapproval, but he ignored her and riffled the pages. Linc picked up a copy of *Dirt Biker* and leafed through it.

Disappointed to find the whole address book unintelligible, Valentine wandered over to one of the windows and peered down on to Warren Avenue. A bus stopped at the corner and several persons emerged. His attention was drawn to a young woman dressed in a pale green uniform and a wide-brimmed blue hat. There was something indefinably forlorn about her. She carried several large books against her breast. The floppy brim of her hat prevented Valentine from seeing her face as she walked across the street and passed directly beneath the window.

"There she is," warbled Susie, "Miss America . . ."

Susie was at Valentine's side with a tray bearing four cans of beer. Valentine and Linc thanked Susie and each took one. Clarisse joined them at the window, and Susie handed her a can, taking the last for herself. She set the tray on top of the television. The young woman with the hat and books entered the beauty salon next door.

"That was Miss America Perelli," Susie informed them. "She's Mr. Fred's sister – the manicurist. Real sweet. Takes care of Mr. Fred like she was Mr. Fred's mama. Actually, Mr. Fred's about fifteen years older than Miss America. Miss America's into geography."

"Geography?" echoed Linc.

"You know," said Susie. "Like 'What's the smallest state?' And 'Where is Yellowstone National Park?' Like that."

"Oh," said Clarisse vaguely. "How interesting."

Susie raised her beer suddenly in a toast to Clarisse. "Hey listen, this is for getting those goddamn gypsies out last night." They drank. Susie motioned the three of them to sit. "Hon, I can tell you I was a little scared when I saw you coming up the stairs with that torch –"

"Torch?" gasped Valentine.

"– but," Susie continued, "Julia said, 'That woman knows her stuff, fo' sure.' "

"Thank you," said Clarisse modestly, sipping her beer.

"*What* torch?" demanded Valentine.

"Oh, this acetylene thing strapped to her back," said Susie. "Looked real professional."

Clarisse shrugged deprecatingly. "Just a little psychological backup. I would never have used it. I didn't have any goggles."

Linc stared at Clarisse.

"She needed it," said Susie in Clarisse's defense. "Why, when they got that credenza out on the fire escape . . ."

"Credenza?" echoed Valentine weakly, putting down his beer. "They got a credenza out on the fire escape?"

"It was just for show," Clarisse reassured him. "It's almost impossible to aim a credenza with any accuracy. It's still out there," she added. "When the workmen come, we'll try to get it back in. It's not a bad piece of furniture. I thought I'd keep some of my books in it."

Valentine shook his head.

Susie took a swig of beer. "And when that old grandmother"—she narrowed her eyes toward Valentine and Linc—"meanest damn bitch ever walked the face of this earth" —she swept her glance back to Clarisse—"when that old bitch pushed the refrigerator down the stairs at you, I thought it was all over. I said to Julia, 'Let's go out there and wipe that poor woman up off the stairs.' "

Clarisse glanced at Valentine, who sat open-mouthed. "The refrigerator didn't hit me," she said. "It got stuck on the landing. Broke through the wall. That's going to have to be fixed, too. Actually, that's why I can't show you *my* apartment. That refrigerator is blocking the stairs and there's no way to get around it right now."

"While you were displacing the gypsies, how did you manage to avoid the boys in blue across the street?" Valentine asked.

"Oh, they came over all right. They said they were behind me one hundred percent, as long as I didn't ask them for any help. All I wanted was to borrow one of those new electric nightsticks and a rubber hose."

"Why wouldn't they help you?" Linc asked.

Clarisse shrugged. "Legalities. They don't like to get involved in tenant-landlord confrontations. Unless there's blood—a lot of blood. Besides," she said with a lively shake of her shoulders, "I could handle it, and the cops knew it, too."

"Do they know this is going to be a gay bar?"

"They put up with the new Eagle and with Fritz. As long as there's no trouble, they don't care. Why should they? I invited them to come over for a drink on opening night."

"What?" Valentine exclaimed. "Why didn't you just ask them to send over the vice squad and pull their paddy wagons up to the door? Clarisse, how do you expect this place to be a success if all of District D comes over? It'll look like we're being raided."

"You could announce that it's uniform night," Susie suggested. "Nobody'll know the difference then."

"What if somebody notices the guns? The nightsticks? The walkie-talkies broadcasting police news?"

"Don't worry. I told them they were welcome as long as they were out of uniform and off-duty."

Valentine was about to say more, but he was suddenly distracted by the sound of a motorcycle approaching with its throttle wide open. The noise roared up to the building and remained as the engine was repeatedly revved up.

"Jesus!" shouted Susie. She put down her beer and went to the window. Pushing aside a hanging plant, she opened the window, then leaned out and shouted, "Listen, Turkey, you stop that noise—"

Valentine and Linc had risen, too, and went to look out the room's second window. The black cyclist was thin and small, wearing denim jeans and jacket, dark aviator glasses, a leather cap, and leather gloves with studs. The driver revved the engine several more times, and then looked up.

"Take a ride on my hog!" the cyclist barked at Susie.

"Don' you talk trash at me, muthah!" Susie screamed back. Pulling back inside the window, she said proudly, "That's Julia. That's my honey. And those are my honey's new wheels."

Clarisse waved down to Julia who gunned the engine again in response. Susie went to the desk and flicked on the telephone answering machine, then flung open a closet door and pulled out a short oxblood leather jacket and a glittery red motorcycle helmet. "You all stay and finish your beers. Nice meetin' you, Daniel, Linc. 'Bye, Clarisse!" And she was out the door.

Valentine, Linc, and Clarisse peered out the window again as Susie appeared noisily on the sidewalk below. She strapped on her helmet, swung onto the back of the cycle, and threw her long slender arms about Julia's waist. With an explosion of exhaust, the motorcycle wheeled around and roared out of sight.

"Aren't they sweet together?" asked Clarisse.

Valentine sighed heavily and put his can aside. "Let's get out of here. I just want to go home and take an overdose of Valium and forget this entire goddamn neighborhood."

"I'd like to see the downstairs again, if you don't mind," said Linc.

They returned to the barroom and Linc looked about the place again, this time even more closely than before. When he was finished, he leaned against the bar, folded his arms and hooked one heel of his boot over the tarnished brass foot rest. He addressed Valentine and Clarisse in a businesslike tone. "It wouldn't take more than five full-time workmen to get this place in shape by the end of the year. That is, if you subcontract the plumbing, plastering, and wiring. It hasn't been abused, just neglected. If you get somebody in here who knows what he's doing, you'll have a real gem on your hands by New Year's. I don't mean just this bar, but the apartments upstairs, too."

"You know five honest hard-working men?" Clarisse asked.

"If I count myself, I do."

"Count yourself," said Valentine. "When can the five honest hard-working men begin work?"

"By the end of the week."

"Is this a ploy?" asked Clarisse with a half-smile.

"What kind of ploy?" Linc asked, surprised.

"Either you're desperate for a job, or you're desperate to hang around my friend Valentine here."

Linc laughed shyly. "I do want the job," he confessed. "Very much. But," he added, glancing at Valentine, "hanging around here might not be so bad either."

"Fair enough," said Clarisse.

"As far as I'm concerned," said Valentine, "you've got the job." He looked once more about the grimy, shadowy room. "You know," he said seriously, "maybe I should have stayed in the hospital. I was happy there with my IVs and my tranquilizers and people waiting on me, and—"

"And no job," Clarisse cut in, "and no future, and no security. There's a chance you can have that now." She waved a hand around, vaguely pointing into the dim corners of the barroom. "*This* is your future."

Chapter Four

VALENTINE and Clarisse moved into their new apartments on a Saturday afternoon three weeks after Linc had first been shown the place. While waiting for the permits to be processed and construction materials for the bar to arrive, Linc and his crew of four put Valentine and Clarisse's apartments into habitable condition. Valentine's kitchen was refitted with new, smaller stainless steel appliances. The depredations of the occupancy of the former occupants were erased from Clarisse's apartment. All miscellaneous pieces of furniture, everything that had not been hurled from the windows on the night of the eviction, were taken out and junked. The rooms were rewired, and new lighting installed in every room. The walls were patched and painted, the floors sanded to a high polish. Following Clarisse's careful instructions, her small second bedroom had been converted into a study with shelves and soundproofing.

Clarisse felt a little guilty that her apartment was so much larger than Valentine's—she had the entire fourth floor to herself. But Valentine said, "I'll be spending all my time in the bar. I don't need more room than this. Besides, I love the idea of living across the hall from a respectable prostitute and her girlfriend. Adds spice."

By the end of the three weeks, necessary city clearances had been obtained for the bar renovations and the selective demolition was begun. As Valentine was returning to the rental truck downstairs for yet another box of Clarisse's clothes, Linc opened the front doors of the bar and beckoned him inside. He appeared to be excited about something, but Valentine couldn't hear what he was saying over the noise of the power saws in the back of the barroom. Valentine followed Linc inside and over to the wall opposite the bar.

Linc reached up and violently ripped off a section of the paneling. "Look what's behind it," Linc exclaimed. Valentine put the carton on the floor and pressed his hand flat against the exposed wall surface. Despite the layers of grime and dust it felt cool and smooth, but he couldn't immediately identify the material.

"Slate," said Linc. "Pure slate. It's just beautiful." He took the kerchief from his back pocket and proudly wiped the exposed slate clean. "Beautiful . . ."

A smile appeared on Valentine's face and grew broad as he drew his hand over the cold, gray surface. "Slate," he said, pleased. "Wouldn't be such a bad name for the place, would it?"

———

———

ABOUT a week later, a little after four o'clock on a Friday afternoon, Valentine sat in the office above the bar. After finishing the apartments upstairs, the workmen had tackled this small space. Valentine decided he would need it long before the bar itself was completed. The walls had been replastered and painted charcoal gray and the floor was covered with off-white carpeting. A glass-shaded floor lamp sat between two easy chairs Valentine had had in his old apartment. On the walls, he had hung three large frames containing playing cards from his own substantial collection. The room was already comfortably cramped, the way the office of a bar always is. A green-shaded desk lamp illuminated papers and checkbooks scattered across the green blotter on the desk. Valentine's chair was swiveled around to face the new one-way mirror that had been installed Thursday. He looked out over the work in progress and saw Slate as it would be if he succeeded in remaining within Noah's budget and Linc's estimates.

Although the workmen had gone home early this first day of the weekend, a lone figure stood below at the bar. It was Paul Ashe. He was leaning with his elbows on the bar, poring over one of the bar giveaway magazines that were already being delivered—in quantity—to Slate. A portable radio sat at one end of the bar, and he tapped his foot in time to music Valentine could not hear. He and his paper were lighted by a single bulb in a wire cage that dangled on a long cord from an exposed fixture in the ceiling.

Ashes, as Paul was generally known, was painfully slender. His black hair and chin-strap beard were heavily flecked with gray. He wore, as nearly always, a black T-shirt and faded blue jeans. One thin bicep was bound with a three-inch-wide band of black leather with three rows of chrome-plated studs. A silver amyl nitrite inhaler dangled from a leather thong tied about his neck. On a left belt loop of his jeans was a heavy key ring, from which two subsidiary rings jangled, each with more than a dozen keys of various sizes and colors. Peeking out of his left back pocket were pointed corners of red, yellow, blue, khaki, and black bandannas.

Ashes had given notice two weeks before at another gay bar in Back Bay to come to work for Valentine. Clarisse had briefly looked askance at Ashes' wasted appearance and his avowed fondness for drugs and the outer, experimental reaches of gay sexuality, but Valentine merely said, "He's got a good head for business and he's helped to set up at least two bars I know about."

Valentine straightened the papers on his desk, put away the checkbooks, and went down to the bar.

"Anything interesting?" he asked when he saw that Ashes was reading the personals in *Jason's Thing*. Ashes contributed a biweekly column on the goings and doings of motorcycle clubs of southern New England. Instead of payment, he received as many free advertisements in the personals as he wanted.

Ashes pointed to one of the small-type entries on the open page of the paper.

" 'Paramilitary Dutch lesbian desires transsexual penpals of all ages. Box 130,' " Valentine read aloud.

"Not that one," said Ashes. "The one right next to it." Relieved, Valentine then read aloud: " '*Wanted: GM, age/race/ looks unimportant, for WS, FFA, humiliation, scat, regurgitation, spit, footwork, verbal abuse, catheters, bondage, bestiality, shaving, initiation and hazing fantasies, hot wax, oil, prolonged immobility, genitorture, simulated operations, and cuddling. Please respect my limits. Box 117.'* "

"Well, Ashes," said a voice from the front of the bar, "still the romantic, I see."

"Who is that?" asked Valentine, peering into the dimness beyond the pool of light.

As the man stepped forward, his silhouette took on substance and color. Ashes' mouth creased tight in displeasure.

Sweeney Drysdale II wore a tweed sports jacket with suede patches at the elbows, a rust-red V-neck sweater, and a solid dark brown velvet bow tie on a wide-striped shirt. His height was just a bit over five feet, his frame was slight and frail, and he bought all his clothes in Jordan-Marsh's boys' department. His hair was blond, thinning, and combed straight over from a left-hand part. On the whole, he looked like one of the "Our Gang" kids gone corporate. He brushed imaginary lint from his gray wool slacks, pushed his large-framed red glasses against the bridge of his nose, and smiled in deliberate hypocrisy.

"Ashes, I just had to stop by after I read your mention of this place yesterday." Sweeney Drysdale swiveled his head around as if he were looking about, but his eyes remained on Ashes. "Of course you made it sound like *Paradise Regained*, but I must tell you that it looks like the Ninth Circle of Hell, illustration by Doré." He leveled his smile at Valentine. "Hello, Daniel."

"Sweeney," said Valentine tonelessly.

"It's gorgeous," said Sweeney without looking around and with a startling intensification of his hypocritical smile. "Who's your decorator? Or perhaps I should ask, have you really found exactly the right person to project your intended image of masculinity coupled with social awareness and a keen appreciation of the good life?"

"I'm pretty much designing it myself," said Valentine, ignoring Sweeney's sarcasm. "With a little help from Ashes here."

Sweeney blinked, paused for a beat, and said, "I'm sure it will be fabulous in the extreme." He took a deep breath, smiled as he held it, and as he exhaled, asked politely, "Aren't you going to show me around your new domain, Mr. Valentine? You and I can leave Ashes here to puzzle out the obscurer abbreviations in the personals. Who knows, Ashes? Maybe you'll find something you haven't tried, though I must admit that seems unlikely . . ."

"Well," said Valentine, hedging and again ignoring Sweeney's barbs, "the place is still pretty torn up. I'm not sure it would be such a good idea to show you around right now . . ."

"That's right," said Ashes, not looking up from his paper. "It would be a real pity if you tripped on a board and a ten-inch nail got driven right through your brain. Or if you accidentally turned on the power saw in the cellar and got your fingers cut off, one by one, and then your arms, and then your feet . . ."

"Exaggeration purely for effect is *so* cheap," Sweeney said, straightening his shirt cuffs. "You *ought* to show me around, Daniel," he went on. "As you well know, my column makes bars." He flicked a speck of lint from his lapel. "And it breaks bars. I'd be careful whose bad side I got on. It's not even Halloween, and this place won't open till New Year's. That's a long time. You could get so much bad mouth in that amount of time that it wouldn't even be worthwhile to open your doors. Hate to see anything like that happen, though."

Ashes was about to say something further, but Valentine placed a hand on Ashes' arm. "So," Sweeney said unexpectedly, "just heard you were having some troubles with your major investor in the place."

"My major investor?" Valentine asked patiently.

"La Belle Lovelace, of course. She's putting up most of the money, isn't she? That's what I hear."

"No, that's wrong."

"Without her you would never have been able to open a place yourself. That's what everybody says."

"Do they?"

"Yes," Sweeney said with a tight smug smile, "they do."

"You know," remarked Valentine wearily, "this is none of your fucking business. So why don't you do us a favor and go away?"

"What?" exclaimed Sweeney in genuine surprise.

"Open the front door," said Valentine. "Step outside. Close the front door behind you."

"And keep walking," Ashes added with a vague smile as he turned the page of his paper. "Go north. That's a good direction. Change your name. Cut off your nose to spite your face."

"You can't—" Sweeney began to protest, now somewhat flustered.

"Can't *what?*" asked Valentine, matching Sweeney's earlier hypocritical smile. "Write what you like in your column—about me, about this bar. We're calling it Slate, by the way. But it doesn't matter what you write, because when I open on New Year's Eve, you'll be here along with every other faggot in Boston."

"I wouldn't count on it," said Sweeney, with a resumption of his dignity. "I just wouldn't count on it." He turned sharply on his heel and swept out of the bar, slamming the door behind him.

Chapter Five

CLARISSE paused in her headlong rush down the stairs as she saw a white rectangle being slid beneath the street door. The paper was given one last flick from outside, and it spun around and came to rest on the newly scrubbed marble tile. She flew down the remaining steps and yanked open the door. A raw wind blew a sheet of rain across her face as she leaned out and looked in both directions along Warren Avenue, but no one was in sight. Clarisse pulled back inside and retrieved the envelope from the floor. She ran one long fingernail under the flap and sheared the paper open. Inside was a card with a gaudy photograph of the Pig Tail Bridge in South Dakota. Clarisse flipped it open and read the typed message.

– – YOU ARE CORDIALLY INVITED – –

TIME: This Thursday, 7:30 – 10:00 P.M.

PLACE: Mr. Fred's Tease 'n' Tint

OCCASION: To Welcome Our New Neighbors

Your Host & Hostess: *Mr. Fred & Miss America Perelli*

Clarisse put the invitation back into its envelope and with her fountain pen scrawled across the front: "We're going. No argument." Then she shoved it into Valentine's mailbox.

Clarisse was about to fling herself out the door when she noticed a letter in her own box. She unlocked it and took it out. It was another invitation to the party. In Valentine's hand, scrawled across the front in green ink was the message: "I'm not letting you out of this one."

———

———

AT the appointed time on Thursday night, Valentine arrived at the Tease 'n' Tint. Mr. Fred greeted Valentine with a broad smile.

The roundness of Mr. Fred's face was emphasized by his large hazel eyes and bushy moustache, and echoed by the rest of his body. His rotundity and the shining clearness of his skin made him appear younger than his thirty-five years; in fact, Mr. Fred looked like a baby pumped full of helium. Mr. Fred Perelli was, moreover, a vision of neatness, from his carefully shaped hair to his carefully starched dark blue smock and highly polished white wing tips. There was a charming hesitancy in his gestures and in his speech; and his eyes were constantly watchful of those around him, as if gauging whether they were happy with him or not. The week before, in a neighborly gesture, Mr. Fred had brought a large box of Italian bakery cookies to the bar for the workmen, and had introduced himself in a neighborly way to Valentine.

"I don't know where Clarisse is, Mr. Fred," said Valentine, now stepping into the shop and looking around curiously. It was the first time he had been inside.

There were only two hair-cutting stations, each with a lime-green Formica shelf and a large circular mirror behind. On one of these shelves was a large glass punchbowl, and the other held an array of liquor bottles and mixers. Miss America's manicure table was against a wall and on it were two ice buckets and a stack of parti-colored paper napkins. There were no other guests, and no sign of Miss America. Valentine asked, "Am I early?"

"You're right on time," said Mr. Fred. "Clarisse is already here," he added, with a gesture toward the door to the back room. Then he said, with a tilt of his head and a glance at his makeshift bar, "I'm flawless with henna rinses, but I couldn't mix a decent drink to save my life. Besides, I'd be nervous fixing a drink for a real bartender."

Valentine nodded absently, for he was looking carefully at Mr. Fred's hair. It occurred to him that it had been a different style the week before. Then he realized that it also had been a different color. "Let me go ask Clarisse what she wants first. Is it all right if I go in back?" Mr. Fred smiled and nodded. Valentine went in to the small back room. On one side was the sink for washing customers' hair, and on the other were several out-of-date dryers. Clarisse was under one of these, the old-fashioned plastic cone pulled down over her head. Her legs were crossed, and she read silently from an open law text resting in her lap. She looked up when Valentine loudly called her name.

"Is Mr. Fred doing your hair?" Valentine asked, surprised. "Raymond's going to be furious."

Clarisse raised the cone. Her hair was dry and she'd pushed it back off her ears with small ornamental combs at each temple. "I didn't have my hair done. I just had to get these last few pages down and this dryer is great for concentration. I know it's rude, but my career comes before politeness."

Valentine shrugged. "There's nobody out there. You and I are the first ones here. I guess the South End doesn't like to be the first to arrive at a party."

At the back of the small room was an aqua curtain, and just then a shadow from behind crossed its folds. Valentine heard the clatter of dishes and a sweet musical humming. Clarisse evidently heard none of it.

She tapped the cone above her head. "These things are great. They're like sticking your head in a vacuum. I'm thinking of buying this old one from Mr. Fred for the apartment."

"Your place is soundproof."

"You tell me that when Susie and Julia are taping 'Battle of the Network Stars' right underneath me."

"What would you like to drink?"

"A Pearl Harbor."

"I'm out of Mídori," said Mr. Fred apologetically, coming up from behind. "And I forgot the grapefruit juice."

"Scotch and water then, Mr. Fred," said Clarisse with a smile. "But that will have to be my only drink of the evening. I have an exam tomorrow."

Clarisse went back to her book, and Mr. Fred followed Valentine back to the bar. As Valentine prepared the drinks for Clarisse and himself, Mr. Fred poured a glass of 7-Up.

"Who else have you invited?" Valentine asked.

"Oh . . . everybody," replied Mr. Fred with a vague smile. "Everybody," he repeated more firmly, as if that were a slightly better explanation.

"Mr. Fred," a light female voice called from the back room. "Would you come help me with the hors d'oeuvres, please?"

"Coming," Fred responded immediately. He took his 7-Up and Clarisse's drink as well, and hurried toward the back.

Alone at the front of the shop, Valentine looked about. The overhead lights had been dimmed, but not enough to relieve completely the effect of purple-flocked wallpaper and lime-green furnishings. Valentine stepped closer to the long wall and examined the photographs of the exotic models displaying three generations of exotic hairdos. The styles of the fifties most fascinated him, and he went down the row of photographs, pausing briefly before each. When he reached the last he took a long swallow of his drink and turned, startled to find Miss America Perelli standing behind him.

"Pick a state," she said with a smile.

Miss America was nearly her brother's height, but slender and pale, with short curly chestnut hair. Her eyebrows were thick, the lashes long, and she was wearing her white manicurist uniform. Pinned just above her left breast was a stickpin bearing the image of Old Faithful above the word *Yellowstone*. Her earrings were tiny lumps of coal, rounded and glazed, with the letters *W. Va.* etched into them. Valentine's first impression of her remained: there was something forlorn about Miss America, as if she had just that moment despaired of ever having the opportunity to hike up the slope of Mount Saint Helens. On a manicurist's tray around her neck was a platter bearing a number of small sandwiches, the crustless bread dyed a rainbow of pastels, and cut into the shape of all the continental United States.

Valentine picked up a pale blue Mississippi and bit into it—cream cheese and chives, also dyed blue, but tasty.

"I didn't mean to make Mr. Fred abandon you out here," said Miss America with a confiding smile. "It's just that I get so nervous when he's around liquor."

"I see," said Valentine blandly, not caring to pursue that matter.

"Mr. Fred used to be a terrible lush," Miss America went on, "but he stopped drinking right after the apartment sale."

Valentine looked over the tray for a second sandwich.

"Try Utah," suggested Miss America. "That's my favorite."

Valentine picked up pink Utah and put it into his mouth—pimento spread.

"You see," Miss America said, "one time I went to visit our aunt out in Worcester—about six and a half years ago, I guess—and I made the mistake of leaving Mr. Fred all alone. Well, Mr. Fred went out and got drunk on Friday night, but then on Saturday he ran out of money. So on Saturday afternoon he dragged all the furniture out onto the street, put up a for sale sign, and sold every stick of furniture we owned. We had wall-to-wall carpeting, and he pried it up off the floor. Then he spent all that money on Saturday night. When I came back on Sunday the whole apartment was empty and there was Fred, passed out in a sleeping bag on the kitchen floor."

"Well," said Valentine uncomfortably, "it looks like he's over that stage."

"Yes. Do you know that it was a *bartender* who got Mr. Fred to go to AA?"

"Is that right?" Valentine replied with vague interest.

"It certainly is. Not only did he get Fred dried out, but they became lovers, too. Unfortunately, it didn't last."

"Nothing does," said Valentine philosophically.

"That's for sure," said Miss America darkly, pushing a yellow Connecticut toward Valentine with an exquisitely manicured finger. "Last year Mr. Fred fell off the wagon and used the rent money to put a down payment on a chimpanzee. I have to keep an eye on Mr. Fred every minute. I hate to have to say it, but Mr. Fred is just not ready to deal with the world on the world's terms. And that's where I—"

Valentine was saved by the bell over the front door. Julia and Susie had come in. "Oh, excuse me," said Miss America, and went to greet them.

Susie wore a severely tailored gold silk outfit designed in the style of a garage mechanic's one-piece coveralls. A patch sewn above the breast pocket read, in crimson thread, *Lube Jobs.* Julia wore jeans, a red flannel shirt, and a many-zippered, -pocketed, and -belted black leather jacket. Her black motorcycle cap was drawn down so low that the brim cast her eyes in deep shadow. Julia's fists were plunged deeply into the pockets of her jacket and her elbows were thrust defiantly out.

"I hate parties," Julia said to Miss America. "I hate meeting new people."

"There's nobody new here," said Miss America mildly, looking around. "You already know Daniel. Clarisse is in the back. And that's it. There's nobody else. I wonder," she went on doubtfully, "if I should have let Mr. Fred plan this whole thing . . ."

"Where's the beer?" said Julia sharply.

"In the refrigerator in back," said Miss America. "Mr. Fred!" she called quite loudly and very suddenly. "Here comes Julia. Give her a beer. Quick."

Julia stalked off.

"Julia's a little upset," explained Susie with a sigh. "She spent the *whole* afternoon down at the bottom of the Harvard pool, and then they told her that the check would probably take six weeks to come through. Julia gets real upset about money sometimes. The problem is—"

The front bell rang again, and several more guests arrived: young women—white, black, Hispanic, and Oriental; overdressed, over-madeup, over-coiffed, certainly over-perfumed—and all known to Susie. In another few moments, Mr. Fred came out of the back of the shop with Julia and Clarisse.

By now the bell over the front door rang continually as guests flooded in. It seemed as though they had waited in the Warren Avenue shadows for the correct, fashionable time to arrive. Several cops coming off duty wandered over to pay their respects. The prostitutes, who seemed to make up nearly all of Mr. Fred's clientele, came. Members of the male leather fraternity—the Rubber Duckies—who availed themselves of Miss America's closest cuticle-shearing, dropped by. Proprietors of several small local businesses, sculptors and painters from the Boston Center for the Arts, and neighbors from the area all came by to drink Mr. Fred's punch and liquor and to nibble at Miss America's pastel, geographical sandwiches.

Valentine brought a fresh drink to Clarisse and seated himself in the chair next to her in a small waiting area near the front.

"I shouldn't have this," she said, sipping it. "I plan to work later on this evening."

"You know," Valentine said, "I wondered if we'd get on each other's nerves living so close together – seeing each other all the time . . ."

"We shared a house in P'town."

"P'town was different," he shrugged. "That's a resort. This is the city. But I see less of you now than when we lived on opposite sides of Boston."

"We're both busy at different things," said Clarisse. "Me with classes, you with Slate" – she paused significantly – "*and* with Linc."

Valentine's brow wrinkled. "You're jealous? I thought you had gotten over all that."

"I couldn't live so close to you if I hadn't," said Clarisse with a little shrug. "I was just pointing out the fact that Linc has all but moved in with you. No, I'm not jealous. Though I have to admit it's disconcerting to hear you two banging in at half past two on a Saturday night, drunk and happy, while I'm up there going blind reading. Where is Mr. Hamilton, by the way?"

"He went to pick up some tile samples. He's been working very hard."

"He's been working hard to please his employer," Clarisse suggested. Then she glanced over Valentine's shoulder toward the door of the shop. Valentine followed her gaze and saw Paul Ashe come in. His arm was around a tall, muscular, handsome moustached man dressed in denim and plaid. Leaving Clarisse to fend for herself, Valentine stood and went over to them.

"Sorry I'm late," said Ashes, "but we had to see a man about a crucifixion."

Valentine smiled and nodded to Ashes' companion.

"This is Joe," said Ashes. "Joe, get me a drink, will you?"

"Oh, sorry . . ." said Joe, jumping to startled attention. He went off in search of the bar.

"Joe's hot stuff," remarked Valentine.

"He's also a good bouncer," said Ashes. "And we're going to need one."

"I don't want to start hiring tricks and trade," said Valentine doubtfully.

Ashes shook his head. "Neither do I. But Joe's good. I worked with him in Newport. He's as strong as he looks—and he always apologizes."

"Apologizes?"

"Apologizes when he throws 'em out. 'I'm really sorry, mister, but you're drunk . . .' Then *wham*, *bang*, out the door. In fact, some people call him Apologetic Joe."

Joe returned with drinks, and as he handed one to Ashes he said to Valentine, "I know I wasn't really invited, 'cause I've never even met Mr. Fred, but Ashes said . . ."

Someone jarred Joe's arm and his drink sloshed onto Ashes' boots. "Oh, Ashes, I'm sorry, I'm so—"

"Just wipe it up," said Ashes casually, and went on talking to Valentine. "I was thinking today that we ought to fasten some heavy chains on the walls—shackles, that sort of thing. That'd be hot."

"Would you like to donate a few items from your extensive collection?"

"Oh, haven't you heard, Daniel?" said a snide voice behind and somewhat below them. "King Burn-Out here is dismantling his infamous medieval torture chamber." Sweeney Drysdale II had pushed through the crowd and was suddenly standing in their midst.

"Does the Society for Historical Preservation know about this?" Valentine asked Ashes with mock alarm.

Joe bumped Sweeney as he rose from the floor, where he had been wiping Ashes' boot dry with a yellow kerchief. "Excuse me."

"I hear," Sweeney went on, looking up and regarding Joe with undisguised interest, "that Ashes is upgrading his life style. Hoisting it out of the gutter, as it were." He turned smoothly to

Ashes. "What are you going to do with that electric chair?" he asked. "And the stocks?"

"Those I'm keeping," said Ashes, looking Sweeney straight in the eye. "Just waiting for the right person to drop by. Who invited you here, anyway?"

"Mr. Fred called me up and asked me," returned Sweeney. "To give the party a little tone." He adjusted his red glasses and looked around the shop. "And it looks as though it could use some. Be sure you read next week's column—I'll have an item in it about famous Mr. Fred's infamous T 'n' T. A big item," he added seriously.

"I didn't see an electric chair down there," said Joe to Ashes. "I saw the stocks, but—"

"It's called hyperbole," interrupted Sweeney with a sigh. "I was hyperbolizing. *Ex-ag-ger-a-ting,*" he explained with a schoolmarmish smile.

Apologetic Joe's expression darkened. He looked down at Sweeney. "I'm sorry to be rude, but why don't you try folding up and disappearing?"

Sweeney was about to frame a reply but stopped when he saw the anger in Joe's eyes. Instead, he shrugged and edged away into the crowd. "See you in the papers."

Joe turned to Valentine and Ashes, all his anger suddenly drained away. "I really hate it when people talk down to me. People see my chest expansion and they automatically talk down to me. People don't talk down to Arnold Schwarzenegger. I'm going for a refill." He moved off toward the bar.

———

———

VALENTINE was finishing a conversation with a District D policeman when Linc appeared at his side.

"You know him?" Linc asked, as the cop moved off toward the bar.

"To speak to," said Valentine vaguely. He checked the wall clock. "What took you so long? I thought you were going to make a simple pick-up."

"The tile place was in Acton. I got caught in traffic on Route Two."

"Well, you're here. Want to go dancing later on?"

"Sure, but we have to do a little business first. I left the samples for the floor tile next door. I have to get the order in tomorrow, so you'll have to make a decision tonight on the ones you want."

"Fine," Valentine agreed. "You know, I was thinking about that today, and—"

"Well," said Sweeney Drysdale II, suddenly appearing beneath Linc's upraised elbow, "eyes of an angel, mouth of a cherub. Body by Nautilus."

He stepped around so that he was pressed against Linc and Valentine. Then he pushed back a little, smiled, and remarked to Valentine, while keeping his eyes on Linc, "Well, if it's not Mr. Right, it's certainly Mr. More-Than-Adequate."

"I thought you'd left," said Valentine.

"My name's—" Linc began.

Sweeney eagerly grabbed Linc's hand.

"Linc. I know. You're the one who's so handy with tools," he said, as his eyes fell heavily from Linc's face and down his body, as if dragged irresistibly toward his crotch. Sweeney's gaze lingered there a moment, just below his eye level. Then he looked up suddenly. "Are those blond tresses naturally curly, or did Mr. Fred give you one of his famous perm- and blow-jobs?"

"You're being vulgar," remarked Valentine.

Unruffled, Sweeney asked, "Tell me, Daniel, do you pay this young man by the hour?"

Linc's mouth dropped, and Sweeney winked at him before stepping away.

———

———

"ARE you having a good time?" asked Clarisse, stopping Linc with a hand on his arm. She had been talking to Mr. Fred, and Mr. Fred had asked her for an introduction to the carpenter.

Linc stopped, and said, "Yes, it's a very nice party."

"Thank you," said Mr. Fred.

Clarisse introduced the two men.

"Oh, I've seen you going in and out next door all day long. You must work very hard."

Linc laughed. "Oh, I do. There's a lot of work to be done before New Year's."

"I'm sure it's going to be wonderful. Daniel showed me what you've done, and the place already looks a hundred percent better. Have you always been a carpenter?"

Linc shook his head. "No. In school I was pre-med. But I decided that I didn't want to have to deal with that kind of pressure."

"Where did you go to school?" asked Clarisse curiously.

"Tulane—all the way down in New Orleans," said Linc. "I had a full scholarship." He shrugged. "I couldn't have afforded to go to college any other way. See," he said, blushing slightly, "my family was very poor—this was up in Lewiston, Maine—and they weren't even going to be able to afford to send me to Orono. So when I got that scholarship, it was like the whole world opening up."

"I bet it was," said Clarisse sympathetically. "Did you like New Orleans? That must have been a bit of a change after a New England mill town."

"A *decaying* New England mill town," said Linc, with a trace of bitterness. "Yes, I loved New Orleans. I came out there. I had my first lover there."

"The first love is always the greatest," sighed Mr. Fred. "It's never the same after the first time."

"No," said Linc seriously, "it isn't. I was really in love, too. I was young, but that didn't matter."

"What happened?" asked Mr. Fred. "Did he die?"

Clarisse looked about uncomfortably. The conversation had suddenly taken a disconcertingly melodramatic turn. She had promised herself that she would have only one drink this evening, but she was now on her third. She wondered if she shouldn't slug down the rest of it and go after another one in order to avoid the remainder of this exchange. No, she decided, she'd stick it out.

"No," said Linc, "but he was into S&M, and I wasn't, so every time he felt he needed it he went somewhere else to get it."

Linc glanced at Clarisse as if he expected her to say something. "Life is very often like that," she muttered.

"He didn't lie about it or make up stories or anything like that, he just told me outright that he was tricking with these S&M people. I couldn't take it. So after I graduated I packed up and I came back to New England—and I became a carpenter."

"What a sad story!" exclaimed Mr. Fred. "Do you still sometimes think about your friend?"

"All the time," Linc said, shaking his head sadly. "In fact—"

Clarisse suddenly threw back the rest of her drink, said, "Excuse me" in a strangled voice, and made her way toward the bar.

Mr. Fred and Linc continued in earnest conversation.

"WHERE is Susie?" Julia demanded of Valentine. "I want to get out of this place."

"Over by the door," Valentine said as he headed that way.

"Let's go," shouted Julia when she was less than ten feet from Susie, who was in boisterous conversation with three friends.

Susie turned, not pleased with Julia's demand. "I want to stay." Susie's three friends seemed suddenly ill at ease with Julia among them.

"Susie, let's go!"

Susie planted her feet firmly on Mr. Fred's purple linoleum floor. "Julia," she said poutingly, "you are acting like a white woman!" Over her shoulder, Susie said hastily to one of her three friends, "No offense, Patsy." She took a deep breath and said with forced calmness, "Go back home if you're tired, Julia, but I want to stay here and con-vene with my co-horts. I'm not tired."

"You're not tired," Julia snapped, " 'cause you don't do nothin' all day 'cept sit at home on your spreadin' ass watchin' TV, and waitin' for that goddamn phone to ring."

Patsy, in defense of Susie, suddenly reached out and yanked the brim of Julia's cap down over her eyes. Blinded, Julia gasped and swung out with her fist. Susie ducked and Valentine caught Julia's arm, bringing it down smoothly into the crook of his elbow. To an unsuspecting eye it appeared a friendly gesture. Susie's three friends scattered into the crowd.

"Susie," Valentine said with calm authority, "take Julia home." He released Julia.

Susie roughly pulled up the motorcycle cap. "Fighting in Mr. Fred's shop," she said in disgust.

"You know I hate meeting people," complained Julia.

Susie's anger melted abruptly, and as they made their way toward the door, she put her arm around Julia's shoulder. Sweeney Drysdale II held the door open for them.

"Come on, honey," said Susie, ignoring Sweeney. "We'll go watch that new wrestling tape I made on Saturday. Big John Studd and the Animal versus the Might Aztec Twins—it's hot."

As they passed, Sweeney sing-songed, "You can lead a whore to culture, but you can't make her think . . ."

"Horticulture?" echoed Julia. "I'll horticulture you, Sweeney Drysdale, you white-meat turkey."

As Sweeney let the door swing shut on the two women, he was suddenly knocked off-balance as Clarisse elbowed him aside, heading toward Valentine who was now standing on the other side of the front door.

"Have you seen this?" she demanded of Valentine, slapping her hand against a folded tabloid newspaper she was holding. "Look what some jerk said about Slate. I can't believe it." She thrust the copy of the *BAR* into Valentine's hands, and immediately took it back. She looked at Sweeney. "I'm outraged," she said to him, in lieu of formal introduction. "I just can't believe anyone would do this."

"What does it say?" Sweeney asked with feigned curiosity.

"Clarisse," said Valentine, indicating Sweeney, "this is—"

"What does the paper say?" Sweeney interrupted swiftly.

" 'Dry Dishes,' " read Clarisse, gripping the paper in one hand, and with her other placed defiantly on her hip. "Whatever *that's* supposed to mean." She took a deep breath and continued: " *The new South End bar,* Slated *to open on New Year's Eve, is being managed by an unemployed social worker and a sadistic drug addict, a perfect combination, I suppose. Will this mean confessionals in the corners? A dungeon in the cellar? . . . Mr. V may be a visual treasure behind somebody else's bar, shirt slit open to the navel for the panting crowd, but what will he manage to accomplish on his own?* He promises me that Slate *will be like no other bar in the city—cruisy and comfortable and check your attitude at the door, please—but if my other sources are correct, that is a promise to rank with* Your check is in the mail *and* I promise I'll pull out . . .' This is despicable." Clarisse lowered the paper and addressed Valentine and Sweeney heatedly. "Not to mention overwritten. Val, this is the *same* man who wrote that you were in the hospital for a nervous breakdown, isn't it?"

"Yes," said Sweeney, "it certainly is. Well, time to circulate. You have a marvelous reading voice," he said to Clarisse as he moved off into the crowd.

"Who was that?" Clarisse asked, looking after Sweeney.

"Have I met him?"

"You want another drink first?"

Clarisse eyed Valentine suspiciously.

"That was Sweeney Drysdale II himself. You just read his column out loud to him."

Clarisse's eyes widened with surprise and then swiftly narrowed
as she wadded up the newspaper. "Get me that drink," she said.
"And a harpoon."

"Sweeney is not worth the harpoon," said Valentine with a
shrug. "Most people don't know who the hell he's writing about
anyway. Come New Year's Eve, they're going to be lined up outside no matter what he writes."

"He makes me ill," said Clarisse. "In fact, he's just given me a
headache. I'm going home for a little quiet."

"Good luck," said Valentine.

"What do you mean?"

"I'm not sure how long Julia and Susie's truce is going to hold
up."

"They're fighting? About what?"

"Same old thing. Julia resents the fact that Susie gets to stay
home most of the day while she goes out and does manual labor."

Clarisse considered this a moment. "Swimming pool repair
and prostitution both have their disadvantages as professions."
She shook her head, and went off to retrieve her law book from
the back room.

There she found, to her surprise, Sweeney Drysdale II
whispering into Mr. Fred's ear. Mr. Fred was laughing. Miss
America was not laughing. "Come on, Fred," Miss America was
saying, "our guests, our guests . . ."

As soon as he saw Clarisse, Mr. Fred's grin faded and he
looked embarrassed. Clarisse knew what Sweeney had been
whispering in Mr. Fred's ear. Mr. Fred said, "Clarisse, this is—"

Clarisse ignored the beginning of this introduction and said,

"America, thank you for a *wonderful* party. Mr. Fred, you're the perfect host." Turning, her eyes grazed across Sweeney, whose hand was uselessly extended. "Goodbye," she said, with a parting smile over her shoulder for Mr. Fred and his sister.

Chapter Six

CLARISSE'S study wasn't a large room. The shelves on three walls and above the door made it seem even smaller, but she called it *cozy*. Her desk and chair faced away from the single window. The floor was thickly carpeted, and the door, covered in cork, served as a bulletin board. When the door was closed Clarisse couldn't even hear a telephone ring in the next room; the study was her sanctum.

Half an hour after she had left Mr. Fred's party, she sat with her elbows resting on the edge of the desk, poring over an open notebook.

A few minutes later she went into her bedroom and took down a brilliant red football sweater from the top of the closet. It had belonged to Valentine's father, but the Boston College letter had been removed and lost years before Valentine had given it to her. Clarisse shoved her hands into the pockets and wandered into the kitchen, wondering if a small shot of whiskey wouldn't calm her so that she could concentrate. While trying to decide whether to pour the whiskey or not, she fished a stale cigarette from one of the packs she'd secreted at the back of her utensil drawer.

She was about to touch the flame of a match to the tip of her cigarette when she flinched violently and very nearly seared her nose. The whole apartment seemed to reverberate with the sound of squealing tires, crunching metal, and shattering glass. She flung the match into the sink and darted to the window. The sparse traffic below moved slowly and without a hitch.

Then there was another crash, and Clarisse realized that the noise was coming from the apartment below. More sounds of skidding tires and breaking glass surged up through the floor.

Clarisse angrily threw the still unlighted cigarette back into the drawer and stalked through her apartment out to the hall, where the noise was even more deafening. She clattered down the stairs to the third floor and repeatedly banged the palm of her hand against the door to Susie and Julia's apartment. The door was finally jerked open by Susie, who had changed into a skintight tennis outfit, hose and heels. In one hand she held a television remote control device. "What?" she screamed over the noise of the television.

Clarisse seized the control from Susie's hand and stabbed her finger down hard on the off button. There was sudden, palpable silence.

"Hey, goddam it!" shrieked Julia from within.

"Clarisse, what're you doing?" Susie demanded. "That was our favorite 'Demo Derby.' That was the Akron Marathon!"

"Kill her!" shrieked Julia from within.

"I'm trying to study!" Clarisse shouted back.

Susie was suddenly jerked aside and the door slammed in Clarisse's face.

Clarisse ran back up to her apartment. By the time she got to her bedroom the Akron Marathon had been replaced—and more than matched—by the voices of Susie and Julia. Clarisse tossed the sweater on her unmade bed, slipped into some walking shoes, and took her fur coat from the closet. She checked herself in the vanity mirror and pulled on her fur hat. She applied a quick coat of lipstick, picked up her text and a notebook from her desk, and swept through the living room. Just as she was going out the door the telephone rang. She closed the door and locked it and started down the stairs.

Curiosity got the best of her, and she ran back up the stairs, frantically unlocked the door, and dashed for the telephone.

"Can you come downstairs for a few minutes?" asked Valentine. "I'm in the office."

"Is this important?" demanded Clarisse. "I mean, is this *really* important?"

"Clarisse," said Valentine earnestly, "your coming down here will virtually ensure total nuclear disarmament."

———

———

WHEN Clarisse entered the office, she found Valentine sitting on the edge of his desk facing away from the door and toward the one-way mirror. Ashes and Linc flanked him. Laid out on the desk were more than two dozen samples of tile in various shapes, materials, and colors.

"I'm leaning toward a gray floor with a white border," Valentine said to Clarisse.

Linc folded his arms. "I still say this burgundy quarry tile would highlight the walls."

"Black," Ashes maintained. "The whole floor should be black."

Clarisse shifted her books from one arm to the other.

"Well," said Valentine, "what do you think, Clarisse?"

"I think that it's almost ten o'clock, and the law library closes at midnight. That's what I think."

"Come on, Lovelace, we're serious. This is an important decision."

Clarisse stook very still, and said, "The gray."

The three men glanced down at the tiles.

"All over?" asked Valentine. "No border?"

"White border," said Clarisse.

"I don't know," said Ashes. "I have this gut feeling about black."

"Black would be perfect," said Clarisse, glancing through the one-way mirror. The lights in the bar were on, casting pools of garish white light here and there amid the construction. Joe wandered about, looking the place over.

"The burgundy's awfully nice," Linc mused.

Clarisse brushed a wave of hair off her forehead. "Burgundy would be spectacular."

"You're not even looking at them, Clarisse," said Valentine.

"Use all of them," Clarisse said flatly. "Go for a confetti effect. It's ten o'clock. In exactly twelve hours I'm taking an oral exam with the toughest professor at Portia. My entire *life* is on the line, and you want me to play pick-a-tile?" She turned on her heel, and said huffily, "I'm going to the library."

Clarisse swept out of the office, banging the door in her wake.

———

———

FORTY-FIVE minutes later Clarisse was seated disconsolately in a dim corner of the library of the Portia School of Law. She stared blankly out the plate glass window at the only twenty-five feet of Mt. Vernon Street that *wasn't* faultlessly picturesque. She had shut her law text and made a neat pile of the several fat volumes she'd dragged out of the stacks. She checked her watch –the library would close in just about an hour–then glanced out the window again. There was Valentine, staring in at her. His black toque was pulled down over his ears. His leather jacket was unzipped and a red woolen scarf was draped about his neck. He motioned for her to come outside.

She gathered her things and went out to the sidewalk.

"How about a drink and a reconciliation?"

Clarisse smiled warmly as Valentine helped her on with her coat. "I thought you and Linc were going dancing."

"Priorities," said Valentine shortly. "I sent him home."

"I want to get pie-eyed," said Clarisse.

Valentine raised an eyebrow. "What about your exam?"

Clarisse shrugged. "What I really need is a night off. *That's* what will do me the most good tomorrow morning."

They walked to Buddies, a bar on Boylston Street near Copley Square, where they alternately danced and downed Black Russians until the lights were brought up at two o'clock. Clarisse, feigning a torn ligament in her right leg, dragged herself in a grotesque limp from the door of the bar to the front of the line waiting for taxis at the curb, and commandeered the next cab that swung by. When they had tumbled into the back seat of the taxi, Clarisse hiccuped, looked at Valentine, and whispered, "Oh, God. I feel a confession coming on."

"I can take it," said Valentine, reeling slightly against the door.

Clarisse looked at him soulfully, with a frown of anguish. "I haven't given up cigarettes," she blurted. "I know I promised, but I can't do it. I smoke every chance I get. Out on the fire escape, out the bathroom window. I go into McDonald's and order a Diet Pepsi just so I can sit there and smoke. I *walk* to class so I can smoke on the way. For lunch I have a peach yogurt and seven cigarettes. Oh, Val, I feel guilty every time I light a match!" In one swallow she finished off the drink that Valentine had smuggled out of the bar beneath his jacket.

Valentine stared out the window, and then back at Clarisse. He stifled a hiccup.

"You're disappointed in me, aren't you?" said Clarisse, despairingly.

Valentine looked out of the window again, and said quietly,

"While you were leaning out the bathroom window, I was hiding in the cellar . . ."

"Smoking?" Clarisse shrieked. "You can't smoke. You'll *die*! You'll get pneumonia again! Where are your cigarettes?" she demanded.

He guiltily reached into the inside pocket of his jacket and pulled out a package of unfiltered Camels.

She snatched them from him, said *"Ugh!"* and flung them out the window. "If I had brought any with me, I'd throw them out too. I promise, I'll stop right now, *for good.*"

The taxi pulled up before the building on Warren Avenue. Valentine paid the driver and helped Clarisse out. She would have forgotten her law text and notebook had he not retrieved them for her.

"Oh, God," she moaned as Valentine fumbled with his keys. "It's two-thirty in the morning and I'm dead drunk." She turned around, facing the street, and fell back against the brick wall. "I'm a disgrace to my intended profession. Why don't you just leave me out here in the gutter? That's where I'm going to end up. In Girl Scouts they taught us how to make a mattress out of old newspapers. I'll be fine."

Valentine got the proper keys into the proper locks and pushed open the door.

"You need a little sleep, that's all. I'll make you some hot milk—"

"I'll throw up."

Valentine led her up the stairs. As they passed the two doors on the third-floor landing, Clarisse arched her head and screwed up her face, as if listening intently. "I guess Susie and Julia made up. All's quiet."

On the top floor, Valentine turned Clarisse's key in the lock, but it wouldn't move. He tried again, and then realized that the door was already unlocked. He pushed the door open, sighed, and shook his head. "You've got to be more careful, Lovelace."

She shook her head. "I am careful," she said. "I *always* lock my door." Then she shrugged, as if it were not worth the trouble of arguing the point.

They went into the apartment.

"See?" she said, throwing her fur coat over the back of a chair. "No bur-gu-lars. I don't have any milk," she added. "I hate milk. Make me a drink."

"Why not?" said Valentine, going into the kitchen.

Clarisse stumbled toward her bedroom. She first kicked one shoe into the room and then the other. Then she went in.

Valentine poured two snifters of brandy and held them in his hands to warm. He went back to the living room. In a few moments, Clarisse came out of the bedroom.

In a low, weary, and surprisingly steady voice, she announced, "It is now a quarter to three in the morning. In the next seven hours, I have to go to sleep, get up, make breakfast, wash my hair, put on my makeup, pick out a suitable outfit, and get halfway across town."

There was something in her voice that made Valentine say, "And . . . ?"

"And," said Clarisse significantly, "there's a strange man in my bed."

Valentine stared at her.

"I'm pretty sure he's dead," she added. "I wish you'd go check."

Valentine swallowed the brandy from both snifters, carefully put down the glasses, and then rushed past Clarisse into her bedroom.

The room was dimly lighted by the streetlamp in front of the building. On Clarisse's bed, with the covers turned down beneath him, lay a fully clothed man. Valentine stepped to the edge of the bed. In the man's left temple was a fairly clean hole nearly the size of a quarter. Dark blood crusted on the pulpy rim of the opening and trailed down the side of the face to a small, coagulated pool in a fold of the pillow. Valentine touched his fingers to the man's wrist, but jerked instinctively away from the cold flesh. He went out of the room, avoiding looking at the corpse's swollen, purple face.

"Well?" Clarisse prompted.

"You were wrong."

"He's *not* dead?" Clarisse said with animated relief. "Well, let's call an ambulance. Maybe—"

"He's dead all right," said Valentine quickly. "But he's not a stranger. That's Sweeney Drysdale II."

Clarisse took a moment to digest this, and then hiccuped. "Oh, damn," she breathed.

Part Two

Part Two

Chapter Seven

IT WAS nearly noon on Saturday. Thirty-two hours had
passed since Clarisse and Valentine had discovered the corpse
of Sweeney Drysdale II. Clarisse felt as if she had aged a month
for every one of those hours. Not only had she dealt with the
police all the rest of Thursday night, she had gone directly from
District D station to her exam at Portia. She had been so flustered
with the discovery of the corpse in her bed that she filled five blue
books in three-quarters of an hour, and wondered, at the end,
what she had written. When she looked back over it, however,
the analysis of the case the professor had presented looked pretty
good. She made a few minor changes, then handed the blue books
in, well satisfied. She returned to Warren Avenue for another bout
of questions from the detectives across the street. On Friday
afternoon she was able to nap for a few hours on Valentine's bed.
The police had taken over her own apartment. That was just as
well, since she had no stomach for going back there yet. She
hadn't liked Sweeney Drysdale II. Nobody else had either, apparently. Still, it wasn't pleasant to find even an enemy sprawled
across your bed, cold and lifeless.

She now stood at the door of Valentine's apartment, her knuckles raised to rap on the wood. For a few moments, however, she remained still, her head cocked toward Susie and Julia's place across the hall. Beneath the noise of what sounded like a hockey game she detected the voices of the two women raised in argument. Unable to gauge the severity of the fight, she shrugged, then knocked several times quickly and lightly on Valentine's door. She turned the knob as he called out to her to come inside.

"Val—"

He shushed her to silence. Wearing a white chef's apron over a red T-shirt and jeans, he stood leaning in the kitchen doorway. He was tapping a long wooden spoon against his thigh.

Linc stood on a rumpled drop cloth, between the two windows, applying a coat of off-white paint to the walls. Like Valentine, he was staring at the portable black-and-white television angled at the edge of the Mission-style dining table.

It sounded like Julia and Susie's hockey game.

Sighing, Clarisse glanced at the screen. It was wrestling.

"Valentine," she said, brushing back a wing of black hair from her forehead, "I really am in a rush."

"In a minute," he answered excitedly. His eyes didn't leave the flickering screen.

"Shhh!" hissed Linc, his brush still poised in midstroke. Paint dripped to the cloth beneath.

Clarisse plopped down into a platform rocker and, leaning back with a creak of the springs, crossed her legs and smoothed out the dark tawny skirt of her tweed suit. She glanced again at the television.

One of the wrestlers was a squat, dark-complexioned man with a pug face and a body that was like nothing so much as a mailbox with broken legs.

Towering over him was his massive opponent. This rugged giant, with a dark blond beard, lighter swept-back hair, a wide, muscular hairy chest, and tight white trunks, had a general presence that would have done credit to Conan the Barbarian.

Clarisse lowered her heel to the carpet, bringing the rocker forward an inch or two. "Who's that?" she asked idly.

"Big John Studd!" replied Valentine in an exaggerated whisper of awe.

"Oh, God," said Linc, "he could pin me to the canvas any day of the week."

At that moment Big John Studd picked up his opponent, twirled him over his head, and flung him into the turnbuckle. The opponent bounced limply back and crashed into the referee, who flipped over the ropes and down onto the floor below the ring.

"Big John Studd is a great athlete," said Valentine. "Big John fights fair. Big John is not afraid of anyone or anything. Big John is a credit to wrestling. Last week Big John Studd pounded Samoan Number Two right into the ground using the old Polish screwdriver."

Big John Studd climbed out of the ring to the wild cheers of the audience.

With a sigh, Valentine went over to the television and lowered the volume. Linc went back to swabbing the wall.

"What's up?" Valentine asked.

"The cops have finally given me permission to go back into my apartment. I'm glad, because I certainly didn't want to have to spend another night on your sofa. It has all the gentle contours of the Great Pyramid at Gizeh."

Clarisse followed Valentine as he went back into the kitchen. He picked up a large red ceramic bowl from a short wooden counter between the refrigerator and the stove and resumed stirring a thick, lumpy mixture swirled with hues of orange, green, purple, and salmon. Clarisse peered cautiously into the bowl.

"Miss America calls this Mr. Fred's Favorite," Valentine explained. "She gave me the recipe yesterday."

"What's in it?" she asked, then went on hurriedly, "no, wait, I don't want to know. Just tell me it tastes better than it looks."

"I hope it does," said Valentine ruefully, and went on with his stirring. "So, how much of a mess did the boys leave upstairs?"

"My apartment," said Clarisse, "looks like a remake of the Great Dust Bowl. They scattered that damn red fingerprint powder everywhere—on everything that was flat, round, or had more than two square inches of surface area. *All* my makeup. *Every* brush, comb, and nail file. They dusted my soap. They dusted my toilet seat. My closets, my drawers, my cabinets, and the insides of the lids of the shoe boxes at the back of my closet. Every time I open a book a red cloud puffs up out of it. I'm going to have to devote all of November's budget to A-One Cleaners. They even opened the refrigerator and dusted my *broccoli!*"

Valentine stopped stirring for a moment. "They dusted your vegetables? Did they think that the murderer lured Sweeney with the promise of a green salad?"

Clarisse sighed. "They were just being thorough, I guess. Anyway, if you'll let me borrow your Hoover, maybe I can be out of your hair by tonight."

Valentine stabbed a thumb toward the narrow broom closet next to the refrigerator. Clarisse opened it and struggled to pull out the bulky, old-fashioned upright vacuum. Leaning it against a counter, she dropped to her knees and began rummaging for the attachments. In the process, several things she couldn't quite identify in the darkness of the closet fell from their hooks above. Something sharp fell on the crown of her head. "The attachments are under the sink," said Valentine suddenly.

Clarisse pulled out of the closet and glowered at him.

"The bags are under there, too," he said. "Sorry. It always takes time to get used to a new apartment."

Clarisse began to rummage beneath the sink.

"While I'm at it," she said, her voice echoing in the cabinet, "do you have any spot remover down here?" She thrust out one hand and splayed her fingers. The day before, all the occupants of the building had been fingerprinted by the police and Clarisse's fingertips were still lightly stained with blue-black ink. "I've tried fingernail polish remover, Lava soap, and Bon Ami, and I still can't get it off."

Valentine looked at his own smudged fingers and said, "Nothing works."

Linc poked his head into the kitchen, holding up a perfectly clean open palm toward them. "Williams' Lectric Shave," he said. "Takes it right off!" He lowered his hand. "Also good for removing gummed price labels from birthday presents, especially off of plastic."

"Thank you for that hint, Heloise," said Valentine.

Linc smiled and retreated into the living room. He dragged the drop cloth around to another section of wall.

Carefully following Miss America's recipe, printed in block letters on a sheet of ruled pink paper, Valentine took several jars of spices from the cabinet and sprinkled generous amounts into the mixture.

Clarisse stood up and looked into the mixture again. It had turned a uniform puce.

"I have to do my clothes later," said Valentine. "Want to keep me company over at the lesbian Laundromat?"

"Not today," said Clarisse as she piled the attachments into a small shopping bag, "I won't be able to think about anything until I've cleaned up the scene of the crime. Besides, I have a paper due day after tomorrow, and I intend to use my Hoover-time thinking out the principal arguments."

Valentine smiled. "Am I detecting a new hardness of heart?" he asked. "No pang of emotion contemplating returning to the apartment where Sweeney was done in? No outrage against the perpetrator of this heinous malefaction? No discomfort that Mr. Drysdale breathed his last in your boudoir?"

"If you must know," Clarisse said as she balled her fist tightly around the straps of the shopping bag, "I'm putting up a very brave front. But the fact is, I'm completely on edge."

"So much on edge that last night you ate two Napoleons for dessert, finished off half a bottle of Cutty Sark, and then passed out in the middle of a 'Twilight Zone' rerun."

"Emotional distress," Clarisse said shortly, dragging the Hoover into the living room.

Valentine followed her, still stirring the mixture in his bowl, but more slowly now, as it seemed to be stiffening. He went around and opened the door for her. Susie stood in the hallway; one hand was raised and poised to knock.

"Can I come in?" she cried, sweeping past both Valentine and Clarisse. "I've just been locked out of my own apartment!" Throwing herself down into the platform rocker, she kicked off her heels and drew one leg up beneath her. She wore gray-flannel slacks and a maroon silk blouse. With her dangling foot, she pumped the chair back and forth violently. She plucked an emery board from the pocket of her blouse and began working it furiously over the edges of her long, sculpted nails. A massive charm bracelet on one wrist jangled madly with the motion.

"Good morning," said Linc brightly.

Susie suddenly jammed her foot against the floor. The rocker stopped immediately; the charm bracelet jangled on.

"If you people are gonna be cheerful," she said darkly, "put a lid on it."

Valentine stood with his hand on the knob of the open door. Clarisse still held the Hoover in one hand, the shopping bag in the other. No one asked Susie what the matter was; her remark hung in the air.

"Julia has two friends," said Susie. "One of them just got married and moved to Charleston—South Carolina? And the other is in Framingham—on a ten-to-fifteen for extortion."

Valentine and Clarisse glanced at each other. Neither said anything. In the pause, there was only the rhythmic sound of Linc's brushstrokes.

"So," Susie went on inexorably, "everybody who comes to see

us are *my* friends. So Julia thinks, 'cause they're *my* friends, she don't have to be pleasant. She thinks that 'cause they are *my* friends, they are trash."

"Maybe she's jealous," suggested Linc. Valentine darted a warning glance at him, but Linc didn't see it. "Maybe she's afraid somebody'll come along and take you away from her. A lot of people get bent out of shape because of jealousy. I know, I've—"

"No woman on this earth is gonna lure me away from Julia," Susie declared. "And she knows it, and she knows all I want is for her to be nice for about five minutes when my friends come over and then she can go in her room and watch some tapes with the earphones. I just told her that she'd be a whole lot happier if she put a little sugar on her tongue when the doorbell rang. I said to her that *I'd* be a whole lot happier if she put a little sugar on her tongue. I said I deserved that. That's when she showed me what the other side of our door looks like."

"Well," said Clarisse, dragging the Hoover out into the hall, "I hope you two work things out."

The expression on Susie's face suddenly changed. She looked up at Clarisse. "Honey?"

"Yes?" said Clarisse.

"When the cops were over here yesterday, they kept asking questions about *you*. Did you know that?"

Clarisse exchanged glances with Valentine and then looked back to Susie. She came back inside the room and propped the Hoover against the doorjamb.

"Susie," said Valentine, "what kind of questions were they asking about Clarisse?"

Susie was about to answer, but her attention was suddenly drawn to the television. " 'All-Star Wrestling' was great today. I just about fell out of my chair when the Animal came on and ate that sparkler. Y'all mind if I switch on 'Creature Double Feature' ?"

Clarisse sighed, and dropped down onto the couch.

"What sorts of questions?" Clarisse repeated as Bud Abbott,

some cartoons, and a monster devouring a woman holding a handbag flipped silently past on the television screen. "Val, did they ask you about me too?"

"They wanted to know if you was datin' Sweeney, honey," said Susie, pushing herself back into the platform rocker.

Clarisse just stared.

Valentine wrinkled his brow. "But they *knew* he was gay. Why would he be dating Clarisse?"

Susie shrugged. Then she turned to Clarisse again. "And then they wanted to know if I heard you say you was gonna off him."

"What!" exclaimed Clarisse with astonishment. "I had never even *met* the man. I didn't even know who he was when–"

"Well," said Linc, "they asked me if I had heard Julia say *she* was going to kill him."

"When Julia and me left the party," Susie continued, "Sweeney said something de-rogatory to me and to my pro-fession, and Julia didn't like it one little bit. Julia doesn't like my pro-fession neither, but she sure won't allow nobody else to jump down on me about it. Julia just said she was gonna remove a certain part of his anatomy, and not use anaesthesia doing it. And then," Susie took a breath, looking at Clarisse again, "they asked me if you ever went fishing or anything."

"Fishing?" echoed Clarisse weakly. *"Fishing?"*

"And used a harpoon or anything," Susie explained darkly.

"Harpoon?"

"Uh-oh," said Valentine.

"What's wrong?" demanded Clarisse, still bewildered.

"Remember?" said Valentine. "When you found out who Sweeney was and that he'd written that article, you were so angry you asked me to find you a harpoon. Somebody must have heard and told the police, and since he was found in your bed–"

"A harpoon!" shrieked Clarisse. "He was *shot*! Nobody's going to kill a man in their own apartment with a *harpoon*! Oh, God," she wailed miserably. "I'm being framed for a crime I didn't commit!

They'll throw me out of Portia Law! I'll end up in Framingham. They'll put me in the laundry and I'll smell like bleach till the day I die. Oh, God! Where was I supposed to have gotten hold of a harpoon!"

"At the Marine Supply Store in Gloucester," Linc suggested mildly.

"Lovelace," said Valentine, "calm down. You and I have an alibi. Remember? Half a dozen people must have seen you at the library that night. The DJ at Buddies who tried to pick me up, he'll remember we were there. And don't forget the cabdriver."

"And I was at home," Linc added between brushstrokes.

"Were you here all evening?" asked Clarisse, turning to Susie.

"I wish we hadn't been," snorted Susie. "I wanted to go out dancing over at the Saint, but Julia said the place would be full of my friends. She was afraid I'd go off and talk to them the whole night and there she'd be left nursing at the bar all alone."

"So you stayed here after you left the Tease 'n' Tint," said Valentine.

"Sure. We watched a rerun of Boom Boom Mancini's heavyweight match. We always do that when we get mad at each other 'cause it's both of our favorite show and we always make up." The file paused on the edge of a nail. "See, this wouldn't have happened, Clarisse, if you had just locked your door up there."

"I *did* lock my door," protested Clarisse. "I *always* lock my door."

"Not the night he was killed," said Valentine. "Remember, it was open when I tried to put the key in."

"I know it was, but I didn't leave it unlocked. For Christ's sake, I've lived in this city for ten years. I don't go off leaving my door unlocked. Which means," she said after a moment of reflection, "that the killer is walking around with a key to my apartment!"

Linc looked back over his shoulder. "Not necessarily. You can pop these old locks with a credit card." He glanced at Valentine. "I've been meaning to tell you to replace them."

"Let's have it done today." Valentine said.

"I'm getting paranoid," Clarisse said in great distress. "I *am* paranoid."

"Maybe," suggested Susie, eyeing the credits for *The Leech Woman*, "the gypsies came back and did it. For revenge—you know, for throwing them out. You could be a marked woman."

"Maybe," said Linc, "somebody thought it was you, and they made a mistake."

Clarisse sat up straight, and said stiffly, "Nobody would ever mistake Sweeney Drysdale for me. Not even in the dark."

"Especially not in the dark," Valentine added.

Chapter Eight

CLARISSE eventually dragged the vacuum cleaner and shopping bag of attachments upstairs. A short while later, Valentine noticed that the door to the apartment across the hall had been propped open. That was Julia's notice of impending reconciliation, Susie explained as she crept back home. Mr. Fred's Favorite was congealing to a rock hardness in the refrigerator, and *The Leech Woman* was reaching its improbable climax. As Valentine sat on the sofa nursing a warm beer, Linc joined him. He stretched out and laid his head in Valentine's lap. Valentine stroked Linc's smooth jaw, and then gently rumpled his curly blond hair.

"Are you worried?" asked Linc.

"Yes, a little."

"I don't think the police really think that Clarisse did it," said Linc consolingly.

"No, of course they don't."

"I mean, she had an alibi. She was out with you."

"For another thing," said Valentine, "Sweeney wasn't killed in her bed. There wasn't enough blood. He was shot somewhere else, and then moved to her bed."

"Does that make any sense to you?"

"No. But that's what the police figure happened. They're out combing the streets for bloodstains even as we speak. Though why anybody would shoot Sweeney in a dark alley, and then drag him up four flights of stairs to a stranger's apartment, is beyond me. No, I wasn't thinking about Clarisse. I was thinking about something else."

"I know," said Linc. "You're worried about the bar. Well, you don't have to be. People will still come. Nobody's going to stay away just because Sweeney got killed upstairs. Nobody liked him, because he was so nasty to everybody, right? And New Year's Eve is more than two months away. Nobody's even going to remember by then."

"I wasn't thinking about that at all," said Valentine.

"Oh," said Linc, disappointed. "What were you thinking about?"

"I was wondering," said Valentine casually, "if Sweeney had an orgasm before he died."

Linc glanced up, startled. "Had a what?"

"I wonder if Sweeney had sex with the man who killed him."

"It might have been a woman," Linc suggested.

"No," said Valentine. "Sweeney was gay, and he had a real aversion to women. If he did have an orgasm beforehand, that pretty much means the murderer was a man."

"Unless the man he had sex with left, and then a woman came in and killed him," Linc went on thoughtfully.

"That wasn't Grand Central Station," said Valentine. "It was Clarisse's apartment. And the front entrance to this building *was* locked. We don't even know how *Sweeney* got in. In any case, I wouldn't mind a gander at the coroner's report."

"You know," said Linc, "even if he had had an orgasm, that doesn't *necessarily* mean that somebody else was there, you know."

"You don't leave a party and break into a stranger's apartment in order to masturbate," sighed Valentine.

They were quiet for several moments, and then Linc said, "Let's talk about something else."

"In the past six weeks," said Valentine, "I've only had one subject of conversation, and that's the bar. I was sort of glad when Sweeney came along and got killed. Now I have something *else* to talk about."

"We can talk about the bar," said Linc. "I *like* to talk about Slate. You know, Val, I'm proud when I tell my friends that you own the bar."

"Clarisse's uncle owns the bar," said Valentine. "I just manage it."

"But he's gay, too, isn't he?"

"Yes," Valentine admitted.

"And you run it. I think it's very important for bars and gay businesses to be gay-owned and -operated. It's a service to the community. Clarisse did a good thing when she got you into this."

"I guess," said Valentine. "I just feel—I don't know—cast adrift. It all happened so fast, and the building still looks like the set for *This Property Is Condemned.*"

"Well, you might be depressed about it," said Linc with a sigh, "but I'm just jealous."

"Jealous?" Valentine echoed skeptically.

"I don't want to be a carpenter forever," Linc said. "I mean, I was working with wood and tile today and I'll be working with wood and tile tomorrow, but when I'm fifty-seven, I don't want to still be working with wood and tile."

"What else would you want to do?"

Linc smiled. "Retail."

"I was in retailing for a while—about eight years ago," said Valentine. "It wasn't all that great."

"Maybe for you," Linc said, "but I've got a plan." He glanced at Valentine, who said nothing, but whose eyes prompted Linc to continue. "Once I get the money up," Linc said, "I'm going to open a shop in the South End. I'm already looking out for the right storefront. The location has to be right—that's the most important thing. That's another reason I'm jealous, because you were *given* these two buildings right here in the South End, the best place to be. I mean, it's practically a gay ghetto now," he said enthusiastically.

"I've noticed," said Valentine. "What sort of shop are you thinking about? Flowers? Antiques? Overpriced clothing? Movie memorabilia? Chic housewares and fancy foods? That's about the gamut, isn't it?"

"Rent-a-Wrench."

"I beg your pardon?"

"Tools," said Linc. "I'll be retailing what I know best: tools and so on. You know how people never seem to have the right tools on hand, so what I'll do is provide a tool rental service, so they don't have to go out and buy the tools they're only going to use once. I'm going to call it Rent-a-Wrench because wrenches are the one thing that gay men *never* have when they need them. The company's motto will be 'A Man and His Plumbing.' Like it?"

"Very much," said Valentine uncertainly.

"I've thought it all out. I don't need much room, just one little storefront with some storage in the back: natural-wood walls, marble counter, old-fashioned cash register, big neon sign in the front window, maybe with a flamingo or something. I'll have the company's logo on all the tools. I'll have hourly and overnight rates, a twenty-four-hour emergency service—"

"For wrenches?"

"Oh, sure, but other tools too, of course. When you've got to have a wrench, you've got to have one."

Valentine smiled and took a long swallow of his beer.

"And once I get going, I'll give carpentry courses and so on." Linc paused and gazed up at the ceiling. "I think it'd be great to stand behind a counter all day in your own place, talking to people who come in, watching people pass along the sidewalk. Join the Gay Businessman's Association, go to all the meetings. You think it sounds too much like a dream?"

"I think," said Valentine, "that before you know it, there's going to be a chain of Rent-a-Wrenches. First a shop on Christopher Street, and then Castro Street, Santa Monica Boulevard, everywhere. And you'll keep going back and forth: New York, San Francisco, Los Angeles, Washington, Chicago, and you'll write every penny of it off on your taxes."

"Are you making fun of me?"

"No. I'm not. I think it's a good idea."

"I've always wanted to be my own boss. Even when I was in school in New Orleans I knew that that kind of education wasn't right for me. I mean, I read Blake and Conrad, but that doesn't help me, not when I'm painting a room or rebuilding a kitchen. You know what I mean?"

"How long were you at Tulane?" Valentine asked. "Did you finish there?"

"Tulane?" Linc asked, slightly puzzled.

"You said you went to school in New Orleans. I assumed you meant Tulane."

"Oh. No. I couldn't afford that. I went to this two-year junior college. I even had trouble getting in there, because of the state residency requirement."

"Why didn't you go to a two-year school in Maine? Why travel all the way to New Orleans?"

Linc seemed uncomfortable suddenly, and shifted on the sofa. Finally he said, "I went down there with a lover. It was pretty good for a while. I got a job days and went to school at night. Then he left me." Linc sighed slightly. "He fell in love with a guy I went to school with and used to study with at our apartment."

"That's too bad."

Linc shrugged. "It was a long time ago. I was too young to have a lover, anyway. He sends me a Christmas card every year, but that's the only time I ever think of him now." He looked up at Valentine and smiled. "All I'm thinking about now is helping you get Slate opened and figuring out how to get Rent-a-Wrench off the ground."

"And speaking of tools," said Valentine, "Ashes was supposed to be here at three. He's probably downstairs waiting. We're going over to the restaurant supply store and look at some equipment for the kitchen. Want to come? We can go by Benton Lock on the way. I really do think I ought to get the locks changed."

Later in the afternoon, Valentine returned to his apartment alone. He found Clarisse running the vacuum cleaner in his bedroom. She snapped it off when he appeared in the doorway.

"I've been having domestic hot flashes all afternoon," she said almost apologetically. "So I thought I might as well do your carpets while I had this thing out." She yanked the plug out of the wall socket and wrapped the cord around the hooks on the handle of the machine.

Valentine looked about. "You made my bed too?"

"The sight of an unmade bed drives me to distraction."

Valentine sat on the edge of it in order to remove his boots. Clarisse seemed to linger hesitantly.

"Yes?" said Valentine.

"I've been going over a few things in my mind . . ."

"I'd kill for a cigarette," said Valentine.

"So would I," said Clarisse.

"What things?" Valentine asked, lying back on the bed. Clarisse leaned over the handle of the machine.

"You and I have an alibi. Linc was at home, or at any rate that's what he told you. Miss America and Fred were trying desperately to get rid of the stragglers. The party that was supposed to end at ten o'clock dragged on till two in the morning."

Valentine wriggled about on the bed, as if he couldn't quite get comfortable. "And Susie and Julia were watching a boxing match, probably at top volume. They wouldn't have heard if the entire Red Chinese army had marched up the stairs, four abreast."

"Right," said Clarisse. "But what about Ashes? He certainly could have gotten in and out without any trouble. Do we know where Ashes was?"

"As a matter of fact, we do," replied Valentine. "He and Joe were carrying on in the cellar snorting coke till their noses bled. Of course they told the police they were 'checking out some new shelving.' "

"So it was either Joe and Ashes or it was Julia and Susie," Clarisse concluded. "I wish we had a suspect whose guts we hated, but we *like* all those people."

"I don't understand why you've narrowed it down to those four."

"Well," said Clarisse, "how else did Sweeney get into the building?"

"That fire-escape ladder at the back of the building is so low that a man lying flat on his back on the ground could reach it. And Linc had been painting the kitchen that day, so my windows were wide open. I'll bet your windows were unlatched too, weren't they?"

"Just the bathroom window," said Clarisse. "But I should have been more careful about that too, I guess. I wonder if that's how they got in?"

"I don't think so. It's hard to maneuver corpses through windows that small." Valentine shrugged. "*Somebody* knew your apartment was empty at that time. And found a way to get into it. I don't think the murderer just wandered around looking for the nearest empty bed to deposit a corpse on."

"But why my place?" asked Clarisse. "Why not yours?"

"Mr. Fred and Miss America introduced us to two hundred people at that party, and every one of them found out that you and I live next door. It wasn't a secret, and anybody looking out Mr. Fred's window could have seen you get in a taxi on your way to the library. They probably didn't know I'd left too." Valentine stood up off the bed, bent over, and yanked back the bed covers.

"Val," said Clarisse suddenly, "why don't we go out for a early dinner?"

He didn't reply, but pulled back the solid top and striped bottom sheets to expose a corner of the mattress.

"Aha!" he exclaimed. "I knew this didn't feel like my mattress!"

Clarisse was backing out of the room behind the Hoover.

"This is a Sealy," Valentine went on. "My mattress isn't a Sealy. But yours *is*."

"The bulb in my refrigerator burned out this morning," murmured Clarisse. "I'd better go buy a replacement."

"Lovelace!"

She stopped in the doorway, averted her eyes, and began chewing on her lower lip.

"You switched mattresses on me, didn't you? This is the murder mattress, isn't it?"

"I couldn't help it!" she blurted. "I couldn't sleep on the mattress where that man got killed."

"But you don't mind sleeping in the same room?"

"Well . . ." she said falteringly. "It's not as if there were any blood on it or anything."

"This is a new low," said Valentine, shaking his head and pulling the covers and the sheets off the mattress.

"I was going to tell you," Clarisse protested.

"When?"

"Eventually . . ."

"Sure, Lovelace."

"Oh, God . . . I feel awful," she stammered.

"Of course you do. You got caught."

"It's a Posturepedic," she pointed out.

He glanced at the label. "I've always wanted a Sealy Posturepedic." He took a deep breath and sighed heavily. "All right," he said, dropping the sheets and covers back onto the bed. "I suppose I've slept on worse. And who knows? In the night, maybe Sweeney's ghost will whisper to me out of the ticking: '*So-and-so did me in . . .*' "

Chapter Nine

ABOUT a week after the death of Sweeney Drysdale II, Valentine and Clarisse received calls from a detective requesting them to make an appearance the following morning at eleven at District D.

On that bleak Saturday morning, they lingered over coffee in Clarisse's apartment until only ten minutes remained before their appointment. Valentine wondered aloud whether they shouldn't take a lawyer with them, but Clarisse declared herself insulted. With a month of classes behind her, she felt she was practically ready for her bar examination already. Then they went downstairs and crossed Warren Avenue.

Immediately to the left inside the narrow double front doors of the police station was a room with five massive desks shoved into a kind of protective compound in the middle. At a couple of the desks officers were filling out arrest reports, and complaining about their partners, their digestions, or their wives. Prominently displayed on the Formica admitting counter was a wooden sign with stenciled lettering that read:

PRISONER VISITING HOURS

2:00 – 3:00 P.M.
8:00 – 9:00 P.M.
3:00 – 4:00 A.M.
No Food, Clothing,
or Other Paraphernalia

"They have visiting hours at three in the morning?" Clarisse asked wonderingly.

Valentine shrugged. "One hour for each shift on duty, I guess."

At one side of the counter a weary-faced policeman listened to three elderly Vietnamese women ranting in their native tongue. At the other end a young female clerk was sympathetically attending to the complaints of an elderly couple from Alabama whose car had been stolen. They were providing the clerk with a minute account of their day's itinerary, which eventually led up to the car's being parked in front of the Boston Center for the Arts, from which space it had been taken.

Clarisse unbuttoned her black wool coat and Daniel unzipped his leather jacket. Clarisse wore a navy-blue skirted suit, which she thought made her look like the aspiring lawyer she was. She had coerced Valentine into wearing a maroon wool tie with his western-style denim shirt.

When the Vietnamese women paused a moment in their frantic chorus, Clarisse stepped up to the desk.

"Excuse me," she said quickly to the officer, "but could you –"

The policeman turned away from Clarisse and barked to one of the uniformed men at the desks behind him: "Where the hell is Sergeant Chanapong? I can't understand a damn word these women are saying!"

At the mention of Sergeant Chanapong's name, the Vietnamese women showered the policemen with another barrage of
chatter. The officer sighed heavily and glanced away from them to
Clarisse.

"Whatta you need?" he asked.

"Sergeant Brosnan," said Clarisse. "We have an appointment."

"To the right, one flight up. Room two-seventeen." He turned
away from them and growled, "Hanson! Put down that damned
crossword and go and find Chanapong!"

Clarisse and Valentine followed the directions to the second
floor and to the frosted glass of the third door on the left. A voice
within loudly mumbled what they took to be an invitation to
enter.

The tiny room had evidently been formed by the partitioning
off of a much larger room. The only furniture was a rectangular
oak table, much too large for the room, with two wooden armchairs on one side of it and two more on the other. Gray morning
light from the single window lighted a patch of the table top,
showing scars in the wood. The only decoration was an official
black-and-white photograph of the governor and lieutenant governor of Massachusetts.

Sitting in one of the chairs on the opposite side of the table
facing the door was a clean-shaven middle-aged man wearing a
three-piece suit. His tie was loose and his vest unbuttoned; he
looked as if he had been trapped behind the table all morning. His
fair complexion had a pinkish cast and his sandy hair was streaked
with gray. He was unwrapping an enormous hamburger when
Valentine and Clarisse entered. A paper container of steak fries
sat nearby on a sheet of paper to absorb some of the grease. An
open container of coffee so cold it didn't steam was set farther
away by a small stack of folders, as if the detective was afraid he
was going to overturn it.

"Valentine and Lovelace?" he asked, looking up, disappoint-
ment in his eyes and in his voice both. "You're on time. I was hop-

ing you'd be late. Everybody's always late. They can't get by the admitting desk. If you had been late," he said with a little reproach, "I could have had my breakfast." He waved a hand for them to sit.

"We've eaten," said Clarisse. "You go right ahead. Please."

"I'm Brosnan," he said, with a smile, and took a bite of the hamburger. "How are you this morning?"

"Fine," said Clarisse.

"Fine," said Valentine.

They waited.

Brosnan continued to eat the hamburger.

"I take it," said Clarisse, "you called us over here to talk about Sweeney Drysdale."

Brosnan nodded, his mouth full. He pointed at the small stack of files in front of him on the table.

"Rauseo . . ." he began, but paused to swallow.

"I beg your pardon?" said Clarisse.

"That was the detective who questioned us last week," Valentine told her.

"Oh, yes," said Clarisse.

Brosnan nodded, and stuffed his mouth full of the steak fries.

Valentine and Clarisse glanced at each other. Clarisse pointedly looked at her watch.

At that moment, the door behind them opened, and Detective Sergeant Rauseo entered the room. He was a dark-complexioned heavyset man in his late thirties. He wore a rumpled white shirt with a coffee-stained tie, and brown suit trousers with heavy wrinkles at the backs of the knees. His black hair was close-cropped. He sat heavily in the chair next to Brosnan and glared at him.

"That was my breakfast," Rauseo said. "You're eating my breakfast. I had that sent up here."

Brosnan swallowed the last of the hamburger. "Sorry." He shoved the fries over toward Rauseo, who pushed them back.

"Now I gotta order some more," Rauseo complained and got up and left the room.

Brosnan grinned after him as he wiped his greasy hands on a napkin. "Well," he began, flipping open the top file. He reached absently into his jacket pocket. "Mind if I smoke?" he asked, but it was clearly no question.

Valentine said impatiently that they didn't mind at all.

As Brosnan took a pack of Kools from an inside suit pocket, Valentine and Clarisse glimpsed his holstered revolver strapped just below his left armpit. He slipped a matchbook from his vest pocket and, taking his time, lighted the cigarette. He drew smoke deep into his lungs and released it slowly, watching both of them.

"Detective–" began Valentine.

"Rauseo'll be right back," said Brosnan quickly.

Clarisse and Valentine began to fidget. Valentine shifted in his chair, and Clarisse uncrossed her legs and then recrossed them the other way.

Rauseo came back in, sidled around the desk, and seated himself beside Brosnan. "It'll be half an hour. I'll starve," he said reproachfully. He glanced at Valentine and Clarisse.

"Don't be so nervous," he said. "Everybody comes in here scared shi"– he caught himself with a quick flick of his eyes to Clarisse and went on–"shirtless, but we're not so bad."

"It's not you," said Valentine. "It's the cigarette."

"I thought you said you didn't mind," said Brosnan defensively.

"We gave them up recently," explained Clarisse, following the Kool from Brosnan's hand to his mouth and back.

Brosnan took a last deep drag, and crushed out the cigarette. "You should have said something." He stood up and went to the window. "My wife gave it up a couple of years ago." He unlatched the window and drew it up a few inches. Crisp air streamed into the room. He sat back down at the table. "Five packs," he said. "*Five packs*. The one thing she said helped her–"

"Sweeney Drysdale," interrupted Clarisse. "He's dead, and you don't know who killed him."

"And you wanted to ask us some questions," said Valentine.

Rauseo drew the files toward him.

Clarisse pulled her coat up to cover her shoulders.

"You want me to close the window?" asked Brosnan.

She shook her head. "Just tell us how we can help you."

"You got some pretty strange characters hanging around that place," said Rauseo, turning a page of the report, without looking up.

Valentine and Clarisse said nothing.

"You know," Rauseo went on, "everybody we talked to about this Drysdale character hated his guts. I mean, really *hated*," he emphasized, glancing at his partner.

"One corpse," sighed Brosnan, shaking his head. "Seven hundred suspects."

"Hell," said Rauseo, "I talked to his mother. Even *she* didn't like him."

Brosnan slipped one of the folders out from the stack that Rauseo was reading and opened it in front of him. Not looking at it, he said, "Mr. Valentine, Sweeney Drysdale came to visit you a few days before he was killed, isn't that right?"

"He wanted to see what I was doing with the bar."

"Did you show him around?"

"No."

"You two had a fight. You both got hot under the collar. You threw him out on the street."

Valentine replied without hesitation. "He was insulting and I asked him to leave. I didn't get 'hot under the collar,' and I didn't throw him out on the street."

"What are you gonna call the place?" asked Rauseo curiously.

"Nightmare Alley," said Valentine. "The way things are going."

Clarisse bit her lip to keep from smiling.

"I like that," said Rauseo, then abruptly continued. "So

Drysdale was on your case before he died, was he? He said some pretty nasty things about you in his column. Got away with it, too, didn't he?"

"Sweeney said nasty things about everybody. He could have found something mean to write about the Easter Seal child."

"He put in his column that you had a nervous breakdown when you were actually in Beth Israel Hospital with pneumococcal pneumonia," Rauseo went on.

"How did you know it was pneumococcal?" asked Clarisse.

"We're detectives," said Brosnan, reaching for the cold, soggy steak fries. "That's damaging, isn't it?" he asked Valentine. "To call a man crazy who's trying to set up his own business? Establish a good credit rating? I mean, you were fired from your last job. You were in the hospital. You were on your last legs, and here's this twerp who tells the world that you're a psychological incompetent. How does that make you feel?"

"I was furious!" cried Clarisse.

"Not you," said Rauseo. "Him."

"I wasn't thinking about anything except trying to get well," said Valentine.

"I tried to get him to sue," said Clarisse, "but he wouldn't do it. Too much trouble," she said, glancing at Valentine with a little leftover reproach.

"And then," said Brosnan, "the same guy comes back and writes a nasty piece about your bar. Trying to kill your business before you've even got your doors open. That's enough to drive a desperate man to desperate measures."

Valentine looked from one detective to another. "If I had wanted to kill Sweeney, " he said quietly, "I wouldn't have done it with a gun because I don't know how to shoot, and I *certainly* wouldn't have done it in my business partner's apartment."

Rauseo made no reaction to this, but only turned to Clarisse. "So there was Sweeney Drysdale, sabotaging the future of the bar in which you had invested heavily. If that bar fails, you stand to lose a great deal of money, don't you?"

"I have no money invested in the bar," said Clarisse. Then she added loyally, "But I have every confidence that Slate will be an incredible financial success. If I did have a few thousand dollars that wasn't already invested in my wardrobe, I'd give it to Valentine in a minute. I could end up one of the ten richest single career women in eastern Massachusetts."

Rauseo nodded and then asked, "What time did you leave for the library that night?"

"About ten," said Clarisse.

He looked at Valentine. "And you met her there?"

"Yes, at about eleven. A little after. What are you getting at?"

Ignoring Valentine's inquiry, the detective went on, "And this whole business about your claiming to be gay."

"Claiming?" echoed Valentine.

"You live in the same building. Last summer you shared a house in Provincetown. Hell, we see you two coming and going together, day in and day out. *And*, Mr. Valentine," Rauseo concluded with a triumphant smirk, "your fingerprints were found on Miss Lovelace's nightstand, on the headboard of her bed, and on the wall above the bed."

Clarisse stared, as if unable to find words for her astonishment.

"I helped her to move her furniture in," said Valentine. "My fingerprints must have been on every damned piece of furniture she has."

"Your place was covered with prints," said Brosnan to Clarisse, as he swallowed some of the cold coffee. "You must have a pretty active social life."

"Besides Valentine," said Clarisse coldly, "there were workmen in and out of that apartment every day for two weeks. And, in reply to the rude implication of your question, may I say that no first-year law student has *any* sort of social life."

"Sorry," said Brosnan, "I wasn't implying anything . . ."

"Aren't you two going to deny that you're actually lovers,"

asked Brosnan, "and that this homosexual business is just a front?"

Valentine groaned.

Clarisse shook her head in increasing wonderment. "I can't believe this. Why on earth would anybody pretend to be gay?" she demanded.

"Because he's opening a gay bar, that's why!" Brosnan exclaimed.

"Pretending he's one of them so they'll come and buy his booze."

Valentine said with Job-like patience, "If you checked to find out what kind of pneumonia I had, then you probably checked out our alibis for that night. So just what the hell are *we* doing here today? Instead of a few of the other seven hundred suspects you mentioned?"

"That seven hundred was an exaggeration," said Rauseo.

"Nobody's off the hook yet," said Brosnan.

"If nobody's off the hook," said Clarisse, "why did you single out Valentine and me to talk to this morning? Why aren't you hauling in lots of other people?"

Brosnan and Rauseo glanced at each other, but chose not to answer the question.

"Unless you're going to accuse us of something," said Valentine, "we both have things we'd like to get done today."

"Maybe you'd just better make sure you've got a lawyer waiting in the wings," sniffed Rauseo.

"By the time all this is settled, *I'll* be a lawyer," murmured Clarisse, slipping into the sleeves of her coat.

Valentine reached into his shirt pocket and took out an engraved business card. He slipped it across the scarred surface of the table.

"This is our lawyer. He pretends that he's gay, too. It's a real racket these days."

Scowling, Brosnan took the card.

Chapter Ten

A S VALENTINE rose slowly in the ancient cage elevator, the cables and the pulleys shook and wheezed and screeched as if they had not been oiled since their installation. When, with a rattle and a sigh, it finally lurched to a halt on the sixth floor of the narrow office building, Valentine threw back the accordion grate and the wooden safety door and stepped onto the landing. He looked around for the fire stairs and decided that that would be his way back down.

He unzipped his brown leather jacket and loosened the gray scarf that had been tightly wrapped around his neck. He glanced down the narrow hallway. Two glass-domed lights hung from the ceiling, inadequately illuminating the dingy gray walls and the chipped linoleum floor. The linoleum perhaps once had had a distinct pattern, but years of wear and patching had obliterated it. At the end of the hall, past four single office doors, sunlight filtered weakly through the dusty panes of a tiny window overlooking West Street. Valentine could hear traffic, construction machinery, and a siren from below. From behind the office doors he heard a telephone ringing, muted murmuring voices, and

a radio playing soft rock. Valentine stepped over to the wall directory and checked his reflection in the glass. He then walked down
the hall and opened the last of the four doors, entering the recep-
tion area of the *Boston Area Reporter*, employer of the late Sweeney
Drysdale II.

"Excuse me—" Valentine began, but then was startled into
silence. The receptionist was Apologetic Joe.

Joe didn't look up. He wore Sony Walkman earphones. The
Walkman itself was propped up in an open desk drawer. Joe was
listening with intense concentration and jotting notes on a piece of
BAR stationery. The clacking of a manual typewriter could be
heard behind a closed door to one of the inner offices.

Valentine shut the outer door of the office, and the vibration
caught Joe's attention. Valentine smiled and greeted Slate's future
bouncer in pantomime. Joe pushed back the earphones, which
slipped gracefully off the back of his head and closed around his
neck.

"Sorry," said Joe, "I didn't hear you. What brings you here?
Can I do something for you?"

"I brought in an ad for Slate," said Valentine. "What are *you*
doing here?"

"I'm recepting," said Joe. "I just started a couple of days ago. I
mean, I can use the extra money till the bar opens—especially
since they've given me a column. You know," he added shyly, "it's
always been my ambition to have a newspaper column, but I
never really thought I'd get it. It's not one of *BAR*'s big columns,
but it's in every week." He tapped his pen on his note pad. "That's
what I was working on when you came in."

"Gossip? Sports? What are you doing?"

"I'm writing the Disco Digest column."

"Disco Digest?"

"I take the most popular songs of the week and I listen to 'em
real carefully," he nodded at the Walkman, "and then I write down
what the songs are about—what they're *really* about."

"I'm not sure I follow."

"Well, I just listened to this song about twenty times before I got the real gist of it. It's about this girl named Gloria—which is actually an alias—who tells everybody that she's real popular. She says her phone never stops ringing, but it never actually rings. Gloria whatever-her-real-name-is is having a nervous breakdown and hearing voices in her head. It's all told by her girlfriend, but you don't ever find out the girlfriend's name, and that's why it's so hard to figure the song out, but the girlfriend is real upset about Gloria's condition." Joe took a breath.

Valentine smiled. "All that is in 'Gloria'?"

"See what I mean? You miss so much if you don't listen. You've got to go beyond the beat and the melody, you've got to listen to the words, the story of the song, There are messages in the music—and that's what Disco Digest is all about."

"I guess," replied Valentine vaguely. He unsnapped one of the large breast pockets of his jacket and removed a medium-sized manila envelope. "I brought a rough layout of the Slate ad, and—"

Valentine was cut off by the sudden appearance of a handsome large-boned woman with thick blond hair. She wore jeans and a crimson sweatshirt with the sleeves pushed up on her forearms. She had an officious air about her and barely glanced at Valentine as she stepped up to the desk and dropped a cassette tape on Joe's desk.

"This is the new People Buying Things tape, Joe," the woman said. Her voice was edged with urgency. "I want a report on every cut for the next issue. I ran it twice myself last night, and it's all about race relations after the nuclear holocaust. Except for one song, and that one's about getting all dressed up and going out dancing."

"Bernie," Joe said, waving a hand toward Valentine to direct her attention that way, "this is Daniel Valentine. Bernie's our assistant editor," he added to Val, completing the introduction.

Bernie's brow furrowed momentarily. "You're Slate, aren't you?"

"Yes," said Valentine, pleased.

"Slate's a good name," said Bernie, smoothing a wayward strand of hair off her cheek.

"Thank you."

"Scene of the Crime's a better one though," the editor said with an impish grin. "It's not too late to change. I mean, just think what kind of publicity Sweeney's already handed you."

Valentine blinked, but said nothing.

"Hold my calls," Bernie said, turning to Joe. "I'm going to think up the nasty replies for the Letters to the Editor–and while I'm at it, I'll think up the letters too. By the way, are you and Ashes coming with the rest of the staff next weekend?"

"We're still thinking about it," said Joe doubtfully. "Something may come up at the last minute," he added vaguely.

Bernie looked at Val. "How about you? Would you like to share in the Advocate Experience next weekend? It'll change your life."

"For the better?"

Bernie looked displeased with the small joke and started to turn away. Valentine stopped her with his voice. "Look," he said quickly, "who do I see about this advertising copy?"

"Vinny's out right now," said Joe helpfully.

"God knows." Bernie sighed bravely. "I do everything else around here."

Valentine removed a five-by-seven-inch sheet of cardboard from his envelope and handed it to Bernie. Joe half-rose from his chair in order to peer at it. Angled across the paper was the name of the bar in scripted black type against a mottled gray background. There was no other information.

"An ad generally advertises," Bernie remarked, and glanced up at Valentine.

"You said yourself," shrugged Valentine, "Sweeney's already put the place on the map. Besides, we're not opening until New Year's Eve. I'll run the ad like this for a couple of weeks. Then I'll include the address, and then the information about the party and so on."

"A teaser campaign," mumbled Bernie, disapprovingly.

"I thought it was more tasteful than a photograph of the corpse," said Valentine.

Bernie glanced at Valentine, then peered at the advertisement a moment more. She said in a low, insinuating voice: " *'Chalk up a hot one at Slate.'* " She looked up and smiled. "How's that for a clever slogan?"

"Very clever," said Valentine impassively.

"Yes," agreed Bernie, "it really is. So look, I'll give this to Vinny and it'll go in next week, just as it is. If there's any problem, he'll call you." Bernie stepped back into the inner office, saying quickly over her shoulder, "Get right on that People Buying Things tape, Joe."

Joe obediently took out the tape that he had been listening to and inserted the new one. "Bernie's a little on edge," Joe explained in a whisper. "She had to write all Sweeney's columns this week. Fashion. Entertainment. *And* gossip."

"I thought Sweeney just wrote a gossip column," said Valentine.

"That was the only column he had a by-line on," said Joe. "The others got pseudonyms. They didn't want to make it look like one person was writing the entire paper—which was just about the case."

"Have you got somebody to take his place?" asked Valentine.

Joe put the earphones back over his ears and pressed the play button. "Don't you know?" he asked, surprised.

"How should I know who's—"

"Because *I'm* Sweeney's replacement," a familiar voice said behind Valentine.

He turned. There stood Paul Ashe, holding a sheaf of yellowed tear sheets. "I thought I heard you out here," said Ashes.

Joe was already making preliminary notes on the first People Buying Things cut.

"*You're* taking Sweeney's place?" Valentine noticed an open office door halfway down the narrow hallway. Ashes must have been inside.

"He'd *die* if he knew," Ashes said with a malicious grin. "If he weren't already dead, of course. Come on in."

Valentine followed Ashes down a short hallway and through a door that still had a three-by-five-inch index card bearing Sweeney's name thumbtacked to it. The office was small and cramped, with a gray metal desk and a filing cabinet taking up most of the space. Ashes had to slide along one wall to get around the desk to his chair. The space there was discolored where, Valentine guessed, Sweeney also must have slid against it many times. The wall also showed light-colored rectangles where framed pictures had been removed recently. These–nearly two dozen –were leaning in a stack against the wall. The photograph on top showed Sweeney smiling broadly, his arm flung about the shoulder of Wayland Flowers. Flowers' puppet Madam had her grotesque wooden face turned up to Sweeney with an expression of open-mouthed astonishment. Valentine removed a pile of books from a wooden chair by the door and sat down.

"It looks like you've just taken over," Valentine said, eyeing the scatter of papers across the desk.

"My first day," said Ashes. He glanced at the tear sheets he was still holding and tossed them into the wastepaper basket. "Honest to God, Drysdale kept anything and everything that had his name on it. I found a file folder with pages torn out of old telephone directories. He had circled his name in green ink on every one of them." Ashes pulled open a drawer and scooped out a handful of small squares of pink paper. "Telephone messages," said Ashes, rolling his eyes. "Arranged by year." He tossed them in on top of the tear sheets.

Ashes continued to burrow into the desk drawers.

Valentine looked idly about. "Is it always so quiet around here?"

"No," said Ashes, glancing at the watch that was attached to his wide, studded wrist band. "But this week's edition went to the printer about two hours ago. And our two star reporters—our only reporters, I should say— are out on a marathon lunch, to see who can eat the most guacamole without actually turning green."

"Is the *BAR* running a tribute to Sweeney?"

"Well, Bernie thought they should, but she couldn't think of enough nice things to say about him that would fill up two whole lines, so they just stuck his picture on the front page with the dates of his birth and death, and what Bernie calls 'a smart black border.' Both tasteful and chic."

"Which Sweeney never was."

Ashes took a deep breath and leaned back in his chair with his feet up on the desk. He put his hands together at the back of his head, and rolled one of the spurs on his boots across a pile of Sweeney's old correspondence, shredding it slightly. "Would you believe me if I said I was sorry Sweeney was dead?"

"To be honest, I'll have to say no."

"Well, I am sorry he's dead. I'm sorry for his parents, I'm sorry for his creditors. I'm even a little sorry for Sweeney himself—"

"But?"

"But nobody believes me," Ashes said with a shrug.

"Who is nobody?"

"Your neighbors across the street," said Ashes.

"Have the police been bothering you?" asked Valentine in surprise.

"They haven't been bothering *you?*"

"Not really. They hauled Clarisse and me in there the other day and insinuated that I'm a closet heterosexual, among other things. They've talked to Linc a couple of times, too. And they are always coming over to talk to Julia, but mostly they want to look at her motorcycle. And they *all* know Susie Whitebread. I don't think they have any leads at all, they're just fishing. How have they been making things difficult for you?"

A slight frown came over Ashes' face. "I don't have an alibi. Joe and I were in the basement that night. We got coked up, and then we wandered over to Charlie's Cafeteria for some food. But nobody saw us, as far as I know—nobody who'd remember us, I mean."

"Are the police talking to Joe?" Valentine asked.

Ashes shook his head. "*I'm* the one they're coming down on. God knows why."

"You know why," said Valentine, looking around the office.

"Why?"

"You seem to have had a motive," Valentine explained. "You wanted Sweeney's job—and you got it."

"This isn't a job. This is a pastime. I can't make enough here to live off of. They'd know that if they ever saw me cash my paycheck at the fruit stand on the corner. Besides, Sweeney was going to be fired anyway."

"Fired? For what?"

"Because he was writing libelous columns, that's why. A lot more damaging stuff than anything he said about you or the bar. He was tracking down *real* dirt."

"What is *real* dirt?"

"Like So-and-So was paid two hundred dollars to wrap a senator in hospital adhesive tape, and it was So-and-So's room-mate who saved the senator from being strangled."

"Was it true?"

"Probably not," said Ashes. "Though you'd be surprised at the number of men in public office who are obsessed with hospital fantasies. Sweeney wrote down stories he got third-hand. And he was too lazy to check sources. He was putting stories like that in the 'blind' section at the end of his column, but everybody knew who he was talking about. He was also going around snapping pictures of people at gatherings when they were acting silly, and he'd run the photo with a caption like 'So-and-So Grabs His Ankles for Fun and Profit'."

"So why didn't Bernie—or whoever is in charge of this place—just fire him?"

"Because gay people have never discovered the joys of a libel suit. So the paper was safe. And Sweeney's column helped sell advertising."

Bernie came to the door and leaned inside. "Have you found Sweeney's last column copy yet?" she asked Ashes.

"No," said Ashes, "and I've looked through everything."

Valentine looked surprised. "Sweeney wrote a column that was never published?"

"He sure did," said Bernie. "And it was all finished except for Mr. Fred's party. He was supposed to turn it in the next morning. I was hoping to run it next week as a kind of memorial. Besides, I had already paid him for it."

"After the way he acted at Mr. Fred's party," said Valentine, "it was probably going to be a lulu."

"Well," said Ashes, sitting up and slamming shut the drawers of the desk, "I can't find it, so I guess we'll just never know for sure, will we?"

Chapter Eleven

IN MID-AFTERNOON on the day before Thanksgiving, Clarisse entered the small office overlooking the bar. In one hand she carried a pair of leather gloves and a soft leather overnight bag. The sash of her tawny camel-hair coat was untied, and underneath she wore dark brown corduroy slacks and a charcoal-gray cable-knit sweater.

Valentine looked up from a pile of bills and advertising brochures scattered over his desk. He glanced at the desk clock and said, "I thought you'd gone an hour ago."

Dropping her bag by the door, she came over to the desk. She scribbled quickly on a scrap of paper and dropped it on the pile of bills before Valentine. "That's my brother's telephone number. In case there's an emergency and you need me back here immediately."

Valentine wadded the slip of paper and tossed it into the wastepaper basket.

"You mean something by that, don't you?" said Clarisse. "You're trying to tell me something."

"Clarisse, I know that number by heart," said Valentine. "You taped it to the fridge yesterday and last night it was on my bathroom mirror. For a while I thought it was some trick who kept breaking in."

Clarisse threw herself wearily in one of the armchairs. She crossed her legs, grasped the arms of the chair, and pressed her head back over the top, as if preparing against the g-force of a rocket blast-off.

"It isn't fair . . ."

"What isn't fair?" said Valentine.

"It isn't fair that all the family holidays should be in the fall and winter—Thanksgiving, Christmas. Indoors. Overheated rooms. Too much food. Not enough to drink. Nowhere to hide. Bars on the windows. Sadistic matrons patrolling the halls."

"You're not going to a state correctional facility, Lovelace, you're going to Beverly Farms. The third richest township in America, I believe you once told me."

Clarisse lowered her head. She smiled a ghastly smile. "It's true, and it's beautiful there. So come with me, Val."

"I told you, Linc and I are spending the day together. Look, you're coming back on Friday. You'll be there less than forty-eight hours."

"Forty-one hours and thirty-five minutes, providing the trains are on schedule. Of course, they rarely are." She got up and moved impatiently about the office. "Where is the Woodworking Wonder, anyway? Where is the man who's stolen your heart—or at least captured your attention?"

She glanced through the one-way mirror. Below in the bar the fan-and-globe lights were turned up bright while an electrician and his assistant, amid a scattering of tools and spools of wire, worked at cutting away a long, narrow section of wainscoting along the back wall between the restrooms and the kitchen.

"He said he had a little job in Brookline this afternoon —rehanging a cabinet or something."

"Did you invite Joe and Ashes for tomorrow?"

"Of course."

"So that's how it's to be," she said despondently. "While I am in remotest suburbia, dispensing artificial cheer to twelve extremely unpleasant persons who have masqueraded for thirty-three years as my relatives, you and Linc and Ashes and Joe are going to be having a wonderful time, lounging around a turkey carcass. Someday," she added wistfully, "when I'm old and gray, I'm going to find out what it's like to have Thanksgiving dinner with a tableful of people I actually like."

"You should have flown to Morocco to spend Thanksgiving with Noah. He asked you to—he even said he'd pay for your ticket."

Clarisse pursed her lips tightly. "I couldn't afford the time away. I have a paper due in Contracts."

"Don't complain to me if you've decided to become a slave to your career."

"I'm not complaining about my career, I'm complaining about my life. Do you know how long it's been since I had a date?"

"Is that a euphemism?"

"It certainly is," replied Clarisse with a grim sigh. "And I'll even bet the four of you are going out dancing tomorrow night."

"We're going to Metro," said Valentine.

"While I'm in the attic room at Beverly Farms, with the wind whistling down the chimney, reading *Pre-Industrial English Sentencing Systems* by the light of a guttering candle."

She sighed, and turned back idly to the window, gazing down at the bar below again. Her eyes narrowed suddenly when she saw a squat, chrome- and black-striped jukebox sitting at an angle against the wall across from the bar.

"What's that?" she asked.

"What's what?"

"That thing that looks like a jukebox."

"That's what it is—a jukebox. It was delivered yesterday."

Clarisse looked at Valentine in surprise. She pointed to the corner of the office, where a number of boxes of stereo components were stacked, still in their manufacturers' crates and boxes. "You spent a fortune on that system. Why in the world do you need a jukebox?"

Valentine shrugged.

"And it shouldn't be down there anyway," said Clarisse. "The wood dust will get into it."

Valentine laughed shortly. "It's never even going to be plugged in."

"If it's not going to be plugged in, why did you order it?"

Turning back to his bills and his advertising brochures, again Valentine merely shrugged.

"How much did it cost?"

"Twenty-five thousand dollars."

"What?!"

"Plus fifteen hundred a month rental. Starting today."

Clarisse closed her eyes and shook her head. Then a thought came to her, and she sat back down in the chair. "Is this like the business where the man in the blue suit and the purple shirt and the white tie comes in and orders a Coke and you give him a Coke and he pays you with a dollar bill and you give him five hundred dollars in change?"

"You got it," said Valentine.

Clarisse pounded the arms of the chair with her fists. "Pay off!" she breathed. "Where did you manage to find twenty-five thousand dollars?"

"Noah had budgeted for it," said Valentine. "There's a separate account book marked 'Incidentals.' "

"Did someone actually approach you and say he would bust you and this place up if you didn't pay protection money? Or was it a little more subtle than that?"

"If we put in the jukebox," said Valentine, "we are assured that a certain Italian family won't lob bombs into the bar after hours discouraging our patrons."

Clarisse grimaced. "I hate all this. You always know that corruption is there—especially in *this* city, but—"

"I know," said Valentine, "it's unpleasant. You're also not used to it."

"And you are?"

"Don't forget, I've been a bartender for a while. At Bonaparte's it was part of my job to give the cop a guided tour of the basement every month. He also got a cold beer and a bulging envelope."

"Oh, no! Do you mean we're going to have to pay off the cops too?"

"Do you really want to know?"

"That answers my question." Clarisse sighed. "The young lawyer gets a taste of real life."

"I want you to pretend you just had amnesia for the last few minutes," Valentine said.

Clarisse thought for a moment, and then nodded. She stood, closed her coat, and tied the sash. She was about to say goodbye when they heard someone come pounding up the metal stairs from below. In another moment the door opened and Ashes came inside.

"You arrived just in time to tell me goodbye," said Clarisse glumly. "I'm going away. You're staying here."

Ashes looked at her strangely, as if he had no idea what she was talking about. "I would have been here sooner," he said uncertainly, "but I stopped in at Fritz for a beer and ran into Linc. He talked my ear off. And then I nearly got run down by a limo that came to pick up Susie Whitebread."

"A limo?" said Clarisse.

"Yeah. I guess she got back on the Birkin Hare payroll."

The Birkin Hare Institute was a long-established and prestigious medical research facility located a few blocks from Slate on the edge of Boston's Chinatown. Ashes' remark made no obvious sense to them. Clarisse was just about to ask him to explain what he meant, but Valentine shook his head very slightly as a warning for her not to say anything.

Then Valentine said, "I thought Linc was in Brookline."

"Rehanging a cabinet," added Clarisse.

Ashes shrugged. "Well, he wasn't. He was over at Fritz, spilling his guts."

"About what?" asked Valentine. "Our sex life?"

"No, unfortunately. He was telling me his life story. Year by year. The only thing he forgot was to ask me if I cared. Thank God he's only twenty-six."

"Twenty-five," said Clarisse.

"Twenty-three," said Valentine.

They all glanced at one another.

"He told me he was twenty-six," said Ashes. "Because he said he'd been a carpenter since he was nineteen—apprenticed to somebody in New Orleans."

"He told me he had to drop out of Tulane when his scholarship ran out," said Clarisse.

"He told me he just went to night school in New Orleans. He said Tulane was so expensive he hadn't even considered it." Valentine glanced at Ashes. "What else did he tell you? About his life."

"Born in Maine," said Ashes, remembering and slowly recounting. "Father remarried. Ran off to New Orleans, hustled for a while. He was proud of that," Ashes added parenthetically. "Had a lover. Lover jilted him. Moved to San Francisco. Had an affair with his shrink. When back to Portland. Father dead. Nursed his stepmother until she died. Moved to Boston. Fell in love." At this last, Ashes looked up at Valentine with a cold smile.

"That's *nothing* like the story he told me," said Clarisse.

"His parents aren't dead," said Valentine slowly. "They're not even divorced."

"Maybe you and Linc should have a little talk during my absence," said Clarisse, getting up and again preparing to go.

"I think so too," said Ashes. "I'm going down to see how Ralph is getting along with the wiring." He bade Clarisse farewell and, yanking the door open again, clattered quickly down the stairs.

"Are you going to talk to Linc?" Clarisse asked. "If he lied to you about those things, he could be lying about other things, too."

"Other things?"

"Like where he was the night Sweeney got killed."

"He was home," said Valentine.

"He *said* he was home," Clarisse corrected. "Not necessarily the same thing."

Valentine said nothing for a moment. He pointedly looked at the clock on the wall. "I think it's time for us to sit down and solve this crime," Clarisse said.

"Fine," said Valentine. "I mean, we have all this free time on our hands. Setting up the bar is nothing. First-year law school—you can do that off the top of your head. So why don't we just go out and do it? Find out who killed Sweeney. It shouldn't take more than a couple of thousand man-hours."

Clarisse sighed. She looked around. As if randomly, she remarked, "Now that I've given up cigarettes, do you have any heavy drugs I could take with me? Some anti-psychotics would be nice."

"I'll talk to Linc," said Valentine, "if you'll talk to Susie."

"About what?" Clarisse asked in surprise.

"Ashes said that Susie was on the Birkin Hare payroll. They do lots of experiments over there, but they're not Masters and Johnson." Clarisse looked at him blankly. Valentine sighed. "I think law school must be turning your brain to mush." Slowly he explained: "What if Sweeney had had something on Susie—in regard to her connection with somebody at Birkin Hare?"

"But if Ashes knows something, then it isn't a secret," Clarisse argued. "And if it isn't a secret, then you can't have blackmail."

"Maybe Ashes read about it in Sweeney's last column," suggested Valentine.

"You told me that that column was lost."

"Ashes *said* it was lost," said Valentine carefully.

Clarisse pondered this. "You know, I've never been completely satisfied with his and Joe's alibi. They were down in the basement. Then they went out to get something to eat, but nobody saw them."

"It's as good an alibi as Susie and Julia's," Valentine pointed out. "Watching 'Demolition Derby,' and not hearing a sound from the room directly above. And they both obviously hated Sweeney's guts."

Clarisse nodded agreement. "While I'm in the emotional wilderness of Beverly Farms, I'll figure a way to pump Mr. Fred about Susie. Only her hairdresser knows for sure." She sat back in the chair and gazed for several moments at the window that looked out over the bar.

"Aren't you going to be late?"

"No," said Clarisse. "I'm sorry to say that no matter how much I put off and put off, the train is always waiting at the station. I was just wondering what you were going to say to Linc."

"About his different stories? I don't know if I care. They're all just stories."

"You're hedging."

"I don't really want to call him on it though," sighed Valentine. "Not yet, anyway."

"Why not?" asked Clarisse.

Valentine looked around the room as if he were embarrassed.

"I know why," said Clarisse. "It's because opening night is less than six weeks away and you can't afford to change carpenters at this point, right?"

"Something like that," admitted Valentine.

"So in the meantime, you'll let him continue to lie to you."

Valentine winced a little. "It's not lying, exactly. It's making up stories about your past. Everybody does that. It doesn't mean anything. Most people have led pretty boring lives. It's sort of nice when they go out of their way to provide some interesting personal history."

"As long as he keeps his prevarications limited to what happened in the distant past," said Clarisse. "As long as he's not lying about what happened this morning, yesterday, and a couple of weeks ago, right?"

"I'm not going out and looking for grounds for divorce, if that's what you mean."

"I didn't know you were married."

Valentine looked more and more uncomfortable.

"We're not. Or at least I'm not."

"But he thinks he is?" asked Clarisse.

"I don't know what he thinks," said Valentine quickly. "When he starts to talk about it, I change the subject. I talk about the bar."

Clarisse was silent.

"What are you thinking?" Valentine asked.

"I'm thinking," said Clarisse, "that this has all the earmarks of an eventual confrontation, and not a pleasant one either. Linc lies to you about the past, and you lie to him about the present."

Valentine didn't answer. "You really are going to be late," he said.

Clarisse got up, kissed him on the cheek, and was gone.

Chapter Twelve

O N THE Saturday immediately following Thanksgiving, a shroud of dark gray clouds was driven in over the city by a raw northerly wind. As the last of a dreary twilight faded into darkness, a steady rain began to fall and, according to the weather reports, would continue well into the next day.

After she'd dressed, Clarisse sat in her darkened living room and listened to a Billie Holiday recording and watched the rain spatter the windows. She experimented with various things to do with her hands now that she no longer smoked. Occasionally the room was bathed with the flashing blue light from a police cruiser arriving across the street. Curses floated up from below as policemen came out of the station into the cold rain.

Clarisse was in a kind of soft and weary mood. She had, that afternoon, finished a paper that had been a difficult assignment. She was particularly pleased with the result, but hoped her confidence wasn't specious. Although grades for midterm exams in her other four courses had been posted on Wednesday evening, she had not had the chance to look at them. She was confident that she had done well but she decided to stop by the school on her way to the PUMA fund-raiser that evening to take a look. She wished now that she hadn't promised Valentine she'd try to question Mr. Fred at the fund-raiser. On the other hand, she told herself, she hadn't been to a nice cocktail party in months, and the cause for the Prostitutes Union of Massachusetts was a good one. Susie had told her the organization was raising money to retain a lawyer for their members. She leaned back and closed her eyes, listening to the music and the rain, and relishing the knowledge that she wouldn't have to see any of her relatives again before Christmas. If she played her cards right, maybe not even until Easter.

CLARISSE'S midterm grades were posted on the bulletin board in the dim hallway of the third floor of the main building at Portia Law. She discovered that she was fifth in one of the courses—the one she liked least—second in another, and first in the two courses that were judged the hardest of the first-year program at the school. Her grin of astonishment and delight faded a little when she turned and found two classmates glaring at her with ill-disguised envy.

She went downstairs to the student lounge, and sat for a few minutes with a cup of coffee; she wanted to savor her victory alone before she went off to the PUMA fund-raiser. Several prominent professors at Portia were well-known supporters of the prostitutes' union. She wondered if they'd be there tonight, and if she could somehow drop it into the conversation that she had been first in the class in both Civil Procedure and Torts.

The pay telephones in the student union were both occupied so she could not call a taxi. She decided to walk down to Beacon Street, where she'd be sure to find a cab.

She took her umbrella and headed back out into the rain. On

the short distance down to Beacon Street, she lost her footing for a moment on a cobblestone driveway. The umbrella wobbled unsteadily, and rain splashed into her eyes. Clarisse swore under her breath and carefully daubed her face dry with a handkerchief. As she went on a few steps she realized that she'd either lost or slipped her right contact lens. She tried to keep her mind on her grades and how happy she really was as she made her miserable way over the slippery sidewalks down the steepest side of Beacon Hill. At the corner of Joy and Beacon streets, through the welter of rain, she hailed the first cab that came by. It didn't stop. Two others ignored her frantic signaling. Finally a taxi detached itself from the stream of traffic and smoothly pulled up beside her. She couldn't read the company name until she had her hand upon the door, and by then it was too late. She climbed into the back of Saturn Four.

All the windows of the taxi were heavily fogged, possibly because of the patchouli incense burning in a little brass container nestled on the opened door of the glove compartment. "Where to?" said the driver. He had a long, equine face that he turned to her briefly. His hair was dark, greasy, and longer than Clarisse's. A young woman sat in the front seat beside him. Her hair was dark and greasy and longer than the driver's. She was doing something that made a peculiar noise, which Clarisse realized after a moment was the shuffling of a pack of cards.

"Where to?" the driver repeated patiently.

"Where to?" said his girlfriend, without looking around. She began dealing the cards on the seat beside her.

Clarisse sighed and fished the address out of her pocket. She tried to read what Susie had scrawled on it, but with her lens missing the address was only a blur, and when she closed the bad eye she could not read it because of the fitful shadows cast by the streaming rain on the windows. She thrust it through the tray in the bulletproof divider, and said, "Take me here, please."

The driver's girlfriend handed the address to the driver, and he briefly switched on the overhead light. The interior atmosphere of the cab seemed to swirl with the incense.

The driver peered at the address, and without a word swerved suddenly back into the line of traffic. At that moment he flicked a switch and the speakers directly behind Clarisse roared into life, playing Jimi Hendrix's Woodstock version of "The Star-Spangled Banner" at full volume.

"Turn it down!" Clarisse screamed, actually hoping the driver would turn it off altogether. He turned it down.

Clarisse settled back into the seat. It was covered in matted fake fur and it smelled of all the rain-soaked passengers who had climbed into the cab. She took a silver compact from an inside pocket and flipped it open. Relying on the illumination of flickering headlights and streetlamps, she held her eye wide apart and revolved her eyeball in search of the lens.

Just when, at last, the reflection of the slipped lens appeared in the mirror, the cab suddenly swerved around a tight corner and Clarisse was thrown sideways in the seat. She began all over again, and in another few minutes she succeeded in getting the elusive lens back into place. She blinked rapidly, held her eyes shut for a few moments, then opened them again. Focused sight returned. She put away her compact, sighed, and sat back.

In the front seat the driver suddenly exclaimed, "Gin!" His girlfriend gathered up the cards and began shuffling again.

"Christ!" breathed Clarisse. She took a tissue from her coat pocket, wiped some of the moisture from a side window, and peered out. They were going up a vast ramp she didn't recognize, passing a massive, unfamiliar building. She lowered the opposite window a little and peered out. The cab took a slow curve, and suddenly all of Boston was spread out behind them.

She said nothing for a few moments. They seemed to be on some sort of major highway, headed out of the city. She leaned forward and peered up at a sign stretched across the five-lane expressway.

93 NORTH

NEW HAMPSHIRE

MONTREAL

She didn't know whether to blame Susie Whitebread or the driver. She dismally reflected that her ration of autumnal good fortune may have been crowded into those grades on the Portia bulletin board.

She leaned forward, and screaming only a little louder than Jimi Hendrix, demanded, "Where the hell are you taking me?"

"Where you said," replied the driver, awkwardly trying to arrange the new gin hand he had just been dealt.

Clarisse sat back and gave herself up to fate.

Eventually the taxi turned onto an exit ramp and Clarisse began to catch glimpses of a few storefronts. Only one was lighted. Half a mile farther, the taxi halted. The fare was a little more than seventeen dollars. Clarisse stuffed a twenty into the slot and quickly got out of the cab. It took off immediately, before Clarisse realized that she didn't know where she was or the name or the number of the place she was looking for. She raised her umbrella and looked around. She had been let off in the parking lot of a discount drugstore. She could see a church up the street a little; behind her, up on a hill, were some old Victorian houses. There was no human being in sight. One car passed, spraying fans of water to either side.

Directly across the street, down which a torrent of water flowed unchecked, was a vast stone building, with only a couple of its large windows lighted. A single yellow bulb dimly outlined a recessed doorway. Above the doorway, carved into a rectangle of gray stone set into the bricks, were the words *Medford Armory*.

A rain-drenched banner hung over the doorway, but Clarisse

couldn't quite make out what it said. She crossed the street, and her heart sank as the letters began to resolve themselves. The sign read:

EIGHT O'CLOCK
ALL FEMALE TAG-TEAM WRESTLING
VERMICELLI TWINS
VS.
THE HARLEM HELLCATS

Chapter Thirteen

CLARISSE closed the umbrella as she tried to peer through the small, square panes of glass set in the wooden doors of the Armory. The glass was fogged and she could discern nothing.

Taking a deep breath, she tried one of the doors. It opened and she went inside. The foyer was a vast square space of marble and dark wood, lighted by a single gooseneck lamp on a little rickety table at the far side. The light palely illumined the face of a sullen-looking young woman in a rabbit-fur jacket who was counting money in a small black strongbox. Clarisse slowly and carefully made her way across the foyer of the Armory, unthinkingly slinging the rainwater of the umbrella to the right and to the left in the rhythm of her steps.

"You're late," said the woman at the table accusingly, as she shaded her eyes and peered into the darkness. "Annie Hindle just *stomped* on Bertha the Baltic Beauty."

"Is this the PUMA fund-raiser?" asked Clarisse tentatively, an uncertain voice in the vast darkness.

"Don't say that!" hissed the woman at the door. "Nobody here is supposed to know!"

Clarisse reached the desk. "It's a *secret* fund-raiser?" she inquired, again with a sinking feeling.

The woman on the desk nodded. "Didn't your invitation say KISS at the bottom?"

"Yes," said Clarisse vaguely, "I guess it did. What does KISS stand for?"

"Keep It Secret Sister," the PUMA representative said in exasperation at Clarisse's ignorance.

Clarisse handed over a twenty-dollar bill, signifying that she didn't want any change. "Just a receipt, in case I'm lucky enough to have to pay taxes this year," she sighed.

"All the good seats are gone," said the doorkeeper, as if she was glad that Clarisse was to be punished for her tardiness.

"It's all right," said Clarisse, "I brought my opera glasses. Just point me the way."

The woman motioned Clarisse around the desk, and with her foot kicked open a set of swinging doors. There was a deeply shadowed passage beyond, but Clarisse heard crowd noises for the first time.

"Just go straight," said the doorkeeper. Clarisse pushed through the swinging doors and followed the increasing sound of the crowd. Eventually, she came to a wall at right angles to the passage. Turning the corner, she saw a black door outlined with bright light. She reached it and pushed it open.

She found herself in a room about the size of two gymnasiums. A boxing ring had been erected in the middle with four large tiers of bleachers all around it. Yellow and white spotlights cut through the smoky air and recorded organ music played loudly in what was evidently an interval between the evening's principal wrestling matches. Through the open-stepped bleachers Clarisse caught a glimpse of the brightly illumined ring and a couple of dark-trousered officials there. Wondering where to go to find a seat, she paused. The place was hot and she opened her coat. Two teenage boys sitting at the top of the nearest tier of bleachers had caught sight of her in her fur and when she opened the coat and revealed the sharply cut dress beneath, they had instantaneously alerted their companions. The entire row of boys turned, leaned precariously over the slender rail, pointed down at her, stomped their feet, and emitted piercing wolf whistles.

Clarisse clutched the coat closed again, and moved hurriedly between two bleachers to the walkway around the ring. The crowd of approximately five hundred saw her entrance.

There were more whistles.

"Clarisse!" someone shrieked from across the ring.

It was Mr. Fred's voice. She look around and saw him directly opposite, in the middle of the fourth row. He was standing up and waving. Two seats over, Miss America was pointing at the empty seat next to her that they seemed to have saved for Clarisse. Beside Miss America sat Apologetic Joe, wearing his Sony Walkman earphones and an expression of intense concentration. He held a felt-tipped pen poised above a small notebook opened on his lap. Clarisse waved and headed toward Miss America and Mr. Fred. As she did so, her coat fell open.

The crowd applauded.

The two officials paused in their conversation and came over to the side of the ring and peered down at her.

With all the dignity she could muster, Clarisse made her way around the ring. Joe caught sight of her and nodded a greeting.

"Why didn't you tell me this was going to be a wrestling match?" Clarisse demanded loudly of Susie, who sat two rows down. Clarisse wriggled down between Mr. Fred and his sister. "I thought this was going to be a smart little cocktail party where everybody goes into the corner between drinks and writes out a discreet check."

"Well," said Mr. Fred cheerfully, "you're here."

"I was all prepared for vermouth and bright conversation with well-known liberals."

"I don't like wrestling either," Miss America confided in a

whisper. She wore a kelly-green knit dress, kelly-green patent leather pumps, kelly-green hose, and a kelly-green Vermont-shaped glass brooch at her throat.

Clarisse pulled open her coat and began to stretch out of it.

Susie, who had been looking all around at everyone, lurched about and in her fake black accent exclaimed, "Child! These natives are gone get restless again 'less you keep them goods under wraps. You hear me?"

Clarisse pulled the coat back on. "I feel just like Bette Davis in *Kid Galahad*—at ringside in my furs. I'd kill for a cigarette."

"I wouldn't say that near a cop these days," said Mr. Fred.

At that moment, Julia appeared and began inching her way toward the vacant seat next to Susie. "There was this huge line," she said, calling excitedly up to Fred and Miss America. "But I got Annie Hindle to sign." She waved her autograph book at them, and then slipped it reverently into a pocket of her black western-style shirt.

"Hello, Julia," called Clarisse.

"Yum, yum," said Julia, pausing to look Clarisse over. "Look at us," she said vehemently. She sat down next to Susie.

Clarisse tapped Joe on the shoulder, but he was so involved in his music that he didn't respond except with a vague smile. "Is Ashes here?" she asked Mr. Fred.

Mr. Fred aimed a pudgy index finger. Clarisse followed it over the heads in front of them to see Ashes sitting in the first row talking with an Oriental woman wearing a combination of bright colors and a small collection of gold chains and bracelets. "He's interviewing Ms. Ben Wah," said Mr. Fred. "She's running for vice-president of PUMA in the upcoming election."

"I do her nails," Miss America confided. "They're three inches long. Mr. Fred says she could perform open-heart surgery without ever lifting a scalpel."

Clarisse turned back to Mr. Fred. He was playing with one end of his moustache and she realized for the first time that it, as well as his hair, was no longer its usual chestnut shade. He caught her puzzled glance.

"Speed-o dye job," he explained, instantly understanding her wondering expression. "Like it?"

Clarisse looked at his blond waves and then asked casually, "What did you mean when you said something about cops a few minutes ago?"

"I want a weenie!" exclaimed Mr. Fred, jumping up. "Who else wants one? My treat," he added. Mr. Fred leaned across Clarisse and Miss America and lifted one of Joe's earphones. Sounds of the Rolling Stones' new album blared out tinnily. "Weenie, Joe?" Fred shouted.

"No!" Joe shouted back, not realizing he was talking above a normal tone. Mr. Fred let go of the earphone and, using Clarisse's thigh as a lever, pushed himself upright. "Susie? Julia?"

"I don't want no weenie," said Susie Whitebread loudly, not even turning around. "Julia don't neither."

"Mr. Fred—" Clarisse persisted.

"I'll be right back," said Mr. Fred, and began moving through the row toward the concession stand.

Clarisse glanced over the audience again. Much of it was Italian, middle-class, and suburban. It was no wonder that PUMA wanted to keep their sponsorship of the match a secret. Susie rose, turned around, and climbed over the intervening row until she got to Mr. Fred's vacant seat. She pointed out to Clarisse the clusters of women who belonged to PUMA. They weren't hard to distinguish.

"Do you have any connection with Birkin Hare?" Clarisse asked Susie abruptly.

"I want a Coke," said Miss America suddenly. She stood up and slipped past Clarisse, ignoring Susie's angry stares.

"Where'd you hear that?" demanded Susie.

"I heard a rumor," said Clarisse. "I was curious."

"A fat hair burner told you that, I bet," said Susie. "A fat hair burner and a skinny fingernail butcher."

"I didn't say that."

"If it wasn't Fred and America who told you about that, then it must have been the cops." Susie lowered her voice and narrowed her eyes on Clarisse. "You been talking to the cops about Sweeney, right?"

Clarisse fished her compact from her coat, snapped it open, and picked at her hair as she talked to Susie. "What's Sweeney got to do with Birkin Hare?"

Susie snatched the compact from Clarisse's hand, snapped it shut forcibly, and tossed it into Clarisse's lap. "You better level with me, honeybunch. You trying to implicate other people so nobody'll think *you* offed that creep in your bed?"

"I'm not accusing anybody of anything," Clarisse shot back. "I wasn't even asking about Sweeney. I was asking about Birkin Hare, that's all. And I'm certainly not working with the police."

"They didn't tell you about me and Sweeney?" asked Susie suspiciously.

"I brought all of us weenies," announced Mr. Fred, returning from the concession stand. He settled into Miss America's vacated seat with a frail cardboard box bearing a pile of steaming hot dogs smothered with catsup, mustard, bright green relish, and chopped onions. A single can of Coca-Cola was angled into one corner. "Have a weenie, Clarisse," he said, thrusting the box at her.

"You eat mine, Mr. Fred."

"Susie?"

"I do not want a weenie, Mr. Fred!" she shrieked. "I told you that!" Without a further word to Clarisse, Susie got up and climbed unceremoniously back down to her seat. Julia stood up and screamed, "Let's get this show on the road!"

There was a little applause. The crowd was getting restless

for the next match. Susie glared up at Clarisse, then turned and said something to Julia.

"What's wrong with her?" Mr. Fred asked, indicating Susie. He moved back to his original place on the other side of Clarisse. "She's acting like a real cat woman."

"I asked her about Birkin Hare and Sweeney," said Clarisse coolly.

"Oh," said Mr. Fred, snapping open his can of soda.

"What about it, Mr. Fred?" Clarisse insisted.

"I can't talk with my mouth full," said Mr. Fred, taking a big bite of his hot dog. "When my mouth's . . . not full," he mumbled, "I'll tell you all about it."

The bell at ringside clanged frantically. The crowd cheered. Susie turned around to say something to Clarisse, but her voice was drowned out. She shut her mouth and looked back to the ring. The referee climbed between the ropes.

"The next match of the evening," he announced into a hand-held cordless microphone, "is a tag-team event between–" He paused significantly.

At that moment there was a loud and echoing sound of a door slamming shut. An expectant murmur ran through the crowd.

Two women–short, firmly built, identical–with close-cropped flame-red hair, red body stockings, and red knee-high lace-up boots entered from opposite corners, jumped up into the ring, and began madly skipping bright blue jump ropes.

"The Vermicelli Twins!" screamed the announcer.

The audience went wild. It rose. It cheered. It screamed its approval. The Vermicelli Twins were hometown girls, Joe shouted to Clarisse over the uproar.

The twins skipped twice around the ring before flinging their ropes into the crowd and setting off two small riots of souvenir hunters. The two women hopped to the center of the ring, and jumped up and down a couple of times on the canvas. The crowd roared in delight.

"Versus," continued the announcer.

The crowd sat down again. It booed. It hissed its disapproval. It stamped its feet out of rhythm.

"The Harlem Hellcats!"

All the PUMA audience members stood up and began screaming.

The Harlem Hellcats slinked in together at one corner of the ring, then separated, one going off to the left, and one off to the right. Their wild manes of bleached blond hair were streaked with black. Their black body suits were dappled with yellow leopard spots. Wedged into their carmine mouths were enormous beef bones, strips of raw meat dangling from the ends. They hissed and clawed at the audience, and then they flung their bones at a knot of teenagers who were yelling the loudest insults at them.

Joe said something more to Clarisse, but she couldn't make it out. She moved over onto the seat vacated by Miss America and pointed to Joe's earphones. He pulled them down about his neck and lowered the volume.

"Sorry. I said that they're actually from Roxbury. But Roxbury Hellcats doesn't have any ring to it at all."

"I do their hair," Mr. Fred told her. "They're honorary members of PUMA."

The announcer introduced the four women to the audience. Clarisse was probably the only person there who had never seen them fight before. Then he introduced the referee, who was donning shin guards and elbow guards at ringside.

"All right," said the referee, climbing into the ring, "I want a fair fight."

At that moment, one of the Harlem Hellcats ran screaming across the ring, grabbed one of the Vermicelli sisters by the shoulders, and flipped her over backward into the center of the ring. Then she jumped up and down on her right hand.

The downed Vermicelli sister screeched in animated agony as the referee barked, "Wait for the bell! Wait for the bell!"

The Hellcat instantly jumped up and backed off, holding her hands up high above her head. "I didn't do nothing!" she pleaded angrily. "I didn't do nothing!"

Clarisse sighed patiently, and then leaned toward Joe. "Why is Ashes here covering a PUMA event? Do the readers of the *BAR* care about this sort of thing?"

"They eat it up." He looked around at the crowd. "There's a photographer here too, somewhere. Ashes got an exclusive interview with Annie Hindle before things got started. Isn't that great?"

"If you say so."

Two officials had now entered the ring and were in heated conversation with the referee and the defiant Vermicelli Twins in the corner.

In this lull Clarisse said, "I wonder what Sweeney Drysdale would have made of all this."

"He wouldn't have dared show up after that last column he wrote," said Joe.

"What!" exclaimed Clarisse.

The crowd again grew anxious for the match to get under way. They began shouting their protest at the still-arguing officials.

"Ashes told Val that that column was lost," said Clarisse quickly.

"I don't know," shrugged Joe. "But I saw it. On Ashes' desk—about a week ago, I think."

"What did Sweeney say?" demanded Clarisse excitedly.

"I don't remember," said Joe.

"Please, Joe, try to remember."

Joe looked at her curiously, thought for a moment, and then said, "Maybe it wasn't Sweeney's last column. But it sure was nasty."

"Was it or wasn't it his last column?" Clarisse demanded in growing exasperation.

Joe shook his head. "It was on plain paper, that's all I remember. But maybe it was an old column, and that's what I'm thinking of. If Ashes said the column got lost, then that's probably what happened. What difference does it make anyway?"

The bell rang. The officials left the ring while the referee swiftly briefed the two teams before stepping back out of the way. The crowd cheered in deafening anticipation.

Clarisse was about to ask whether the missing column had been on the desk in Ashes' office or the desk in Ashes' apartment, but it was too late. Joe's earphones were back in place. Miss America was suddenly beside her, wanting her seat back. Ashes himself was coming into the row from the other side. Clarisse moved over and gave her seat back to Miss America.

In return for the second Coke Miss America had brought him, Mr. Fred held out a cold hot dog across Clarisse's lap. "You want the last one?"

"You eat it, Fred," said Miss America.

"I'd feel guilty," he said without conviction.

"Think of all the starving hairdressers in India," said Clarisse, pushing the hot dog, dripping mustard and relish, back toward Mr. Fred. She looked to her right and found Ashes smiling a silent greeting to her from the other side of Apologetic Joe.

In the ring, one of the Vermicelli Twins lowered her head into a battering ram, rushed up behind the Harlem Hellcat, and propelled her into the turnbuckle. The Hellcat bounced back and landed face up on the mat. The second Vermicelli sister lifted her leg high and brought her boot down with considerable force on the Hellcat's exposed neck. The Hellcat jumped up and staggered helplessly about the ring making choking noises, while she was mercilessly pummeled by her opponent.

"Give that bitch a mini-pile driver!" shrieked Julia, jumping up and shaking both fists at the Vermicelli Twins.

Clarisse turned to Mr. Fred and insisted, "I still want to know about Susie and Birkin Hare. You've finished eating, so now talk." Clarisse took a cue from Miss America: you sometimes had to be firm with Mr. Fred.

Mr. Fred didn't speak at once. He looked past Clarisse to his sister, who had heard Clarisse's question. His sister glanced back, and gave one short nod of permission.

Clarisse saw this exchange and said, "Thank you, America, now maybe I'll find out something around here."

"Susie was a secretary at Birkin Hare," explained Mr. Fred with a little sigh of resignation.

"A secretary? Susie Whitebread?" Clarisse glanced down with surprise at the back of Susie's head.

Carefully daubing a bit of spilled relish from his chin, Mr. Fred crossed his legs and leaned confidingly toward Clarisse. "Well, that was her job title, anyhow," he went on, warming to his subject. "There was this real important scientist at Birkin Hare, and he was a three-hundred-pound tub-ola. So he went on a diet and he got down to a hundred and forty-five, and he was so happy that he started picking up girls in the Combat Zone. Isn't that what straight men do when they lose a lot of weight?"

"I don't know," said Clarisse. "I have no idea."

"Anyway, one day he met Susie, and he just fell head over heels. He couldn't 'date' her often enough. But he was running out of money, paying for Susie's cabs and things." Mr. Fred was a great one for euphemisms. "So when he couldn't afford it anymore he put Susie on his payroll as a secretary. It seems he had all these research grants, and he put her down as his secretarial help. She was getting paid every week by the Antivivisection League. I know because I used to cash her checks." Mr. Fred, eyeing yet another hot dog, took a breath. "She went to Hawaii once, and once to Palm Springs. Well, this scientist was so proud of himself that he told one of his friends in his laboratory, and then his friend started doing it, and all of a sudden there were secretaries on everybody's payroll, *if* you know what I mean."

"I know exactly," said Clarisse.

With a flying kung-fu-type maneuver, one of the Vermicellis landed a boot hard on the chin of a Hellcat. The crowd roared, but Clarisse was barely aware of what was happening in the ring, so intent was she on Mr. Fred's story. He had to wait till the noise of the crowd died down before he could continue.

"This was when Sweeney Drysdale used to be the afternoon bartender down at the Hungry Eye in the Combat Zone, where all the secretaries hang out. And it wasn't long before he found out what was going down. So when the scientists dropped into the Eye, Sweeney let them know he knew exactly what they were up to with the secretaries."

"In other words, he was blackmailing them," said Clarisse.

"Yes," said Mr. Fred, frowning at the baldness of the word. "And not just the scientists, he blackmailed the girls, too. It's grand larceny when you get on a payroll under false pretenses. Grand larceny is a tough rap," added Mr. Fred, with the air of imparting a lesson to the lawyer-to-be. He took a bite of another hot dog—before it got cold, he explained in a mumble. Then he took up the thread of the story again. "But when Sweeney tried to blackmail Susie, Julia found out about it—this was right after they started living together. Julia saw six shades of scarlet and got some of her girlfriends together one day and they went down to the Hungry Eye and they told Sweeney off like nobody's business."

"They told him off?" asked Clarisse. "That was it?"

"Actually, they pulled him across the bar and smashed a lot of beer bottles over his head. Oh, *and* Julia broke his arm in two places—she just twisted it around behind him till the bones snapped. She also threatened to stick her glue gun in his mouth and pull the trigger. She said after she finished with him he'd better never spread dirt again in his life."

Clarisse looked at the back of Julia's head, and frowned.

"So," Mr. Fred resumed, pausing once more to swallow the last of his hot dog, "Sweeney blew the whistle like a banshee on speed. All hell broke loose. Three of the scientists were fired on the spot, and Birkin Hare had to give back all the grant money. A major *scandale*, even though it was kept pretty hush-hush. All the girls lost their jobs, of course. They tried to beat Sweeney up again, too, but he had hired a bodyguard, and they couldn't get near him. The bodyguard's name was Rosa. Real sweet, but needed to lose some weight. A major *scandale*," he repeated, in conclusion.

"I'd say so," said Clarisse. "Did the police ever find out that Sweeney had been blackmailing all those people?"

"It never went to court. Birkin Hare made sure of that," said Mr. Fred. "They had had enough bad publicity already. But it didn't leave any good feelings between Susie and Julia and Sweeney. Which was hard on me, because I was friends with everybody."

"When did all this happen?"

"About five years ago. Right after Julia and Susie moved in next door."

Clarisse was about to respond when the entire audience rose to its feet, shouting. Bewildered, Clarisse stood on tiptoe to see what was happening in the ring.

Two white-coated attendants, who had raced to ringside, were strapping one of the Vermicelli twins onto a stretcher. She was writhing and screeching and trying to get loose, but they hoisted the stretcher and headed quickly out of the arena. One of the Harlem Hellcats leaped onto the referee's back and got her hands over his eyes so that he was blinded. She gouged her heels into his sides and rode him around and around the ring. Her screeching partner flung the second Vermicelli twin into the ropes. The dazed young woman was shot back with such force that she turned a flip in the air and landed in the Harlem Hellcat's arms. The Vermicelli recovered her senses instantly, wriggled her way to a standing position, seized the Hellcat, and flung her out of the ring. She fell to the floor at the feet of a knot of large Italian women who screamed and slapped savagely at her with their net bags. Her partner leaped from the back of the referee, grabbed the ropes, and jumped down out of the ring. She rescued her partner. The Hellcats and the remaining Vermicelli twin fled into the darkness between the bleachers toward the dressing rooms.

The fans were on their feet in an ecstasy of cheering, whistling, and catcalling as the timekeeper furiously rang the bell. Clarisse used the sudden commotion to edge out past Miss America and Mr. Fred. She made her way around the back of the bleachers, and was about to step into the darkened corridor that would take her back to the lobby, when a strong hand suddenly clutched her sleeve. Clarisse turned in surprise. It was Susie. Susie leaned forward, and for a few moments her breath was hot in Clarisse's ear as she whispered to Clarisse over the tumult of the crowd behind them. Clarisse stood stock still. Her eyes widened, and her mouth fell open. When Susie was done she pulled back, and looked Clarisse straight in the eye.

"You're positive?" said Clarisse.

Susie nodded once, then turned abruptly away. She strode back toward the ring, and did her part to increase the crowd's noise by shouting alternately, "Foreign object!" and "Check it out, ref!"

Clarisse made her way back to the main lobby and out to the rainy street. She raised her umbrella and began waiting for a taxi to pass.

Chapter Fourteen

TWENTY-FIVE minutes later Clarisse emerged from a taxi at the corner of Berkeley and Chandler streets, about two blocks from home. She slammed the cab door shut and walked to the side entrance of the bar called Fritz.

Inside, Clarisse marched straight to the bar and ordered a vodka and tonic. She took a stiff swallow of it as soon as it arrived and before the bartender had brought her change, and then made her way toward the back of the long, narrow room. It was Saturday night, but so many people had gone away for Thanksgiving that the place was uncrowded and relatively quiet.

She found Valentine sitting on the cushioned banquette that ran the length of the outside wall beneath the smoke-tinted windows. Linc, directly across from him, was raptly playing a video game on a table machine. The silver-gray Levelors were lowered but open. Outside, the streetlamps shone murkily through the mist of rain. The twisted limbs of a thriving honey locust scraped against the windows now and then.

Valentine rested one foot on the edge of a low oak table in

front of him and idly watched Linc's score on the machine mount. He took a swallow of his bourbon and glanced up as Clarisse dropped her umbrella on the table, opened her coat, and dropped down wearily beside him.

"Hi!" said Linc, but did not look up.

"Your fur is very wet," he remarked. "Was the fund-raiser held out-of-doors?"

"No," she said.

Something in her voice prompted him to ask, "It wasn't quite what you thought it would be?"

"No, it wasn't quite what I thought it would be. I never before connected fund-raisers with severe personal humiliation. In other ways, however, it was quite revealing. What did you two end up doing this evening?"

Valentine glanced at Linc, absorbed in the game. "We went over to the Cyclorama. A friend of his was singing in the AIDS cantata—the part of the homosexual Haitian hemophiliac who comes on near the end and gives everyone hope." He shook the ice in his nearly empty glass. "Did you talk to Mr. Fred?"

"Did you talk to Linc?" she asked. She finished off her drink when Valentine didn't answer. A passing waiter took their order for another round.

At last finishing his game, Linc looked up and saw Clarisse. He smiled. "I get absorbed," he apologized.

"Here are some quarters," said Valentine, fishing them from his pocket. "Keep at it for a while. Clarisse and I have to talk."

Linc took the quarters with a bright light in his eyes.

In a low confidential voice Clarisse told everything—or nearly everything—that she had learned at the wrestling match. Valentine paid for the drinks when they were brought.

"So what do you think?" she asked when she finished.

"I don't think either Julia or Susie would kill Sweeney because of something that happened five years ago."

"The desire for revenge never dies," said Clarisse.

"Of course it does. Maybe not as quickly as love or sexual desire, but it fades with time, just like everything else. You can't hold a grudge for five years."

Clarisse appeared offended by this observation. "I don't know about you, but I certainly can. And have. And do."

"I know," said Valentine. "But I don't think Julia and Susie have quite your . . . strength of character. If they were going to kill Sweeney, I think it would be for something he did to them that night. And as far as I know all that he did to them that night was to insult them. Of course, maybe he was blackmailing them again."

"About what?"

"I don't know," said Valentine. "But you know how protective Julia is. She doesn't even like Susie to have friends."

"Unless they have thick wallets and don't mind opening them after half an hour's acquaintance," Clarisse pointed out.

"And even if it was Julia or Susie," Valentine went on, "they wouldn't do it in their own building. That would be too stupid."

"All right then," said Clarisse thoughtfully. "But let's think about it. There may be something we haven't quite figured out yet." She told Valentine what Joe had said about seeing Sweeney's column on Ashes' desk. "But he was confused, and couldn't be sure if it was actually the *last* column or not."

"Sweeney saved everything," said Valentine, "so it might have been the draft of an earlier column. But I think we ought to get it straight one way or the other."

They sipped at their drinks. "There are a few other things we have to get straight tonight, too," Clarisse said.

"What else?" asked Valentine.

Clarisse just smiled. Without even looking in that direction, she reached across the table and placed her hand atop Linc's on the controls of the video game machine.

"Hey!" he cried in protest. His hang glider smashed into a utility pole and burst into brief video flame.

Turning with a smile, Clarisse said, "Game's over. We'd like to talk to you for a few minutes."

"Sure. What is it?"

"Please sit over there," said Clarisse, pointing to a chair on the opposite side of the table. Linc got out from behind the video machine and slipped into the chair she'd indicated. "Something's come up," Clarisse said pleasantly.

"About the bar?"

"No. About you."

"Me?" He glanced questioningly at Valentine, who suddenly seemed uncomfortable. Linc then looked back to Clarisse.

"In the past month, as far as Val and I know, you've told at least three stories about your past life. All of them different. So we've been wondering which one of them was true. The one you told me, the one you told Ashes, or the one you told Val."

Now it was Linc who was uncomfortable. "I don't know what you're talking about."

"We're talking about your past—what your life was like before you moved to Boston and became a carpenter."

"Why?"

Clarisse pondered this for a moment. "Stories about people's pasts are a little like job recommendations. They don't actually matter very much if they're true, but if they're false they become pretty important."

Linc glanced from side to side. "You think I lied to you?"

"We think you told three different stories," Valentine put in diplomatically.

"Boston is a small town," Clarisse said flatly. "People talk. If you don't tell the truth, you get caught up. Did you ever live in New Orleans?"

"Yes," said Linc.

"When?" asked Valentine.

Linc glanced away. He replied quietly, "The summer after my freshman year at the University of Maine. I came out there."

"But you didn't go to Tulane," said Clarisse.

"I did go there. One day. On the bus."

Valentine and Clarisse nodded.

"And you had a lover there, who was into S&M," Valentine said after a moment.

"He wasn't exactly my lover. Actually we just had a few dates—just sort of fooled around. He wanted me to put handcuffs on him. He told me he loved me and wanted to marry me—ceremony and everything," he added with quiet incredulity.

"California?" inquired Clarisse.

Linc sighed and shook his head. "My parents took me to Disneyland when I was seven."

"And they're not divorced?" asked Valentine.

"They have problems."

"So do you," murmured Valentine.

"Are they poverty-stricken?" asked Clarisse.

"No," said Linc. "They're rich. They're both psychiatrists."

"I might have guessed," said Valentine.

"In other words," said Clarisse, draining the vodka in the glass, "none of what you said to any of us was true."

"The truth was *boring*," Linc maintained. "You didn't want to hear about my rich psychiatrist parents. You didn't want to hear that I went to the University of Maine at Orono for four years. You didn't want to hear that I spent three months in New Orleans and got laid exactly five times."

"Five times?" asked Valentine in surprise. "That's all?"

"All in August," said Linc glumly. "Listen, I wasn't trying to hurt you or anything. I wasn't trying to put one over on you or anything. I was just trying to . . ."

"To what?" Clarisse prompted.

"To make myself seem more . . . experienced. Does this mean you hate me?"

"Of course not," said Valentine. "But I don't like being lied to, either."

"Nobody does," said Clarisse with a sigh.

Slouched in his chair, Linc looked from one to the other. Clarisse signaled the waiter for refills for Valentine and herself, then pointed at Linc. "And a Miller."

"Don't bother," said Linc, getting to his feet. "I'm taking off. I'll come by tomorrow morning and pick up my tools and my clothes. I won't ever bother you again."

"Sit down," said Valentine. "You're not leaving me without a master carpenter when the bar opens in five weeks."

"But I can't—"

"Yes you can," said Valentine. "And you will. We have a deal, and you're a businessman and I'm a businessman, and we both have a big interest in seeing Slate open on time. If you don't finish this job, it's going to be known all over town that you reneged. If you do finish it, and finish it right, it will mean a whole lot more work for you."

They were silent for several moments. The waiter brought their drinks. They all reached for them greedily. Clarisse paid.

"Is there any chance you'll forgive me? Both of you?"

"Of course," said Clarisse. "I never hold grudges."

"If you promise not to lie again," said Valentine. "You know it takes less energy to tell the truth than it does to lie."

"I promise," said Linc, holding up his hand in the Scout's pledge. "Never again."

"Now that we've got you here on a truth-telling binge," Clarisse began in a businesslike manner, "tell us why you met with Sweeney Drysdale after Mr. Fred's party. Just before he got killed."

"What!" Linc and Valentine exclaimed in unison.

Clarisse glanced at Valentine. "That's another thing I found out tonight. Susie said that after she and Julia got home from Mr. Fred's party that night, they looked out the window and saw Sweeney and Linc down on the sidewalk."

"It wasn't me!" said Linc excitedly. "It must have been somebody else. It was dark, she couldn't have seen . . ." His voice trailed off under their insistent gazes. "It was me," he admitted.

"But Sweeney and I were just talking. I mean, we'd just met, so we were just talking."

Valentine and Clarisse silently looked at him.

He went on carefully: "You said you were going over to the library to look for Clarisse, and I said I was going home—and I had planned to. But when I got out on the sidewalk, there was Sweeney. He was out in front of Mr. Fred's—waiting for a taxi or something—and he called my name."

"What did he want?"

"To talk."

"About what?" asked Clarisse suspiciously.

"He said Mr. Fred had told him about my plans for Rent-a-Wrench, and he thought it was a great idea." His voice inadvertently brightened, recalling the compliment.

"So you stood out on the street talking about *hardware*," said Clarisse. "For how long?"

"I don't know. We went for a walk."

"Where?" demanded Clarisse.

"Around—around the South End."

"Where did this walk end up—his place or yours?" said Valentine.

"Or mine?" added Clarisse with a grimace.

"Back at Slate," said Linc weakly. "We went back to Slate. He said he had a roommate. My place was on the other side of town."

"Why the hell would you want to do anything with Sweeney Drysdale in the first place?" demanded Valentine.

"I did it for you!"

"For me?" Valentine echoed incredulously.

"He said that when he was in the bar the first time he didn't get a chance to really look the place over," Linc said quickly. "He told me he wanted to see the whole building. He said that he'd write it up in his column, tell how I'd done all the renovations and what a good job it was—and he'd say that I was going to open

Rent-a-Wrench. It would be free publicity for everybody. He said we'd all benefit if he put it in his column."

"All this," said Clarisse carefully, "on condition that you and he . . . fool around?"

Linc nodded and said in a low voice, "Yes."

Valentine shook his head.

"But I didn't do anything to him!" Linc cried.

Clarisse ignored this and asked, "Why did you choose *my* apartment to do it in?"

"I knew that Joe and Ashes were down in the cellar, and I was afraid they might come up to the office if we went in there." He looked miserably at Valentine. "I couldn't take him to *your* apartment because . . ." He shrugged helplessly.

"Because you didn't know when I'd be back, but you knew Clarisse was planning to be at the law library until at least twelve," Valentine concluded for him. "Did you card the door open?"

"I still had the keys from the renovation," said Linc. "I forgot to give them back."

"How long were you up there?" Clarisse asked.

"Five minutes. Maybe ten," said Linc, and then added hastily, "but we didn't even go into the bedroom."

"Where did you do it then?" demanded Clarisse.

Linc wiped perspiration from his forehead. "On your couch."

Clarisse turned to Valentine. "Tell that waiter to bring me the Yellow Pages. I want the name of the nearest emergency upholstering service."

"We didn't have sex on it," Linc protested. "I mean . . ."

"Mean what?" asked Clarisse.

"You mean," said Valentine, interpreting, "that Sweeney had sex, and you just sort of looked down and watched, right?"

Linc nodded miserably. "But I didn't do anything to him," he repeated.

"You left the building together?" asked Valentine.

"I took him down to the landing, and I went into the office.

He went on down and out."

"He must have gone back upstairs," said Clarisse.

"I didn't hear him go back up. I don't know how he got back up there. I didn't do any—"

"Stop saying that," Valentine insisted.

"I'm telling the truth!"

"How long were you in the office?" asked Clarisse.

"Five minutes. Ten minutes. I packed up the tiles to take them back to the store. And then I went down to the bar and just looked around."

"What about Joe and Ashes?" asked Clarisse.

Linc shook his head. "The trapdoor was closed, and I couldn't hear anything. But they could still have been down there. I left by the front door to the bar." He got up unsteadily and lurched off, muttering, "I have to go to the bathroom."

Clarisse and Valentine were silent a moment, then Clarisse asked, "So, do we drag him over to District D?"

"All we know is that Linc got him into the building," said Valentine glumly. "We don't know if Sweeney hid at the bottom of the stairs and then went back up, or if he left and was brought back in by somebody else. Either way, what could he have been after in your apartment?"

"I don't know," said Clarisse. "It doesn't make any sense. Of course, Linc could be lying again."

"I don't think he is. It's just that there are still a few pieces missing."

"Yes," Clarisse sighed, "such as a motive—and a murderer."

She put her drink down. "I'm going to go. I don't think I want to be here when he gets back." She paused for a beat, and then asked, "Are you depressed?"

Valentine smiled slightly. "No, I'm not. I didn't say anything to him because he felt bad enough as it was, but nothing turns me off more than lying. It's the one thing I don't think I can forgive." Clarisse pushed back the cuff of her coat, and studied her watch for a moment. Valentine went on: "I have to keep him on for the sake of the bar, of course, but he won't be warming the other side of my bed much anymore. That's all right, though. It's hard to manage a new career and a love life at the same time." He took a swallow of his drink. "It's one less problem that I have to deal with."

"One minute, four and a half seconds," Clarisse announced. Valentine looked at her questioningly.

"That's how long it took you to rationalize the failure of your latest love affair. You're getting better. It used to take you nearly five minutes to dispel the trauma. Five minutes plus two fast drinks."

Valentine swallowed the remainder of his bourbon.

Linc came out of the bathroom, but instead of returning to the table he went toward the bar.

"I'm leaving too," said Valentine. "I've had enough of Linc for tonight." They rose together. Clarisse waited at the door with her back to the room while Valentine spoke briefly with Linc once more. Then Valentine and Clarisse went out into the rain.

"What's the verdict? Are you and Linc going to patch it up with Band-Aids and string?"

"I don't think so. All I wanted was a promise that he'll be in on Monday morning. He said he would."

Valentine snapped open the umbrella over their heads, and they trudged off toward Warren Avenue.

"Will he be in?"

"I reminded him that finishing this job properly was a major stepping-stone on the road to Rent-a-Wrench."

They had reached their corner when Valentine stopped suddenly. "I'm not ready to go home yet."

"My God, you're not even going to give your bedroom a single night to cool off? Are you afraid that if you don't have two people holding down the bed, it'll snap shut with you in it?"

"You're welcome to come with me," he said politely. "I was thinking of the Eagle."

"What? To the Eagle?" Clarisse cried. "And get dizzy watching the video screen go up and down every two and half minutes? Get my eardrums punctured with last year's Top Ten amplified to a hundred and ten decibels? Get trampled by the stampede of men running to the restroom every time somebody they don't like walks in the door, which is about as often as the screen goes up and down? And then, after all that, get abandoned when you do find somebody to mend your broken heart?"

"Sounds like a good time to me."

"You go on. I'll be all right. I've got two hundred and thirty cops within hailing distance if someone tries to attack me. Just leave me the umbrella."

Valentine nodded, relinquished the umbrella, and bade her good night. Cinching up his coat over his head, he headed across the bricked expanse at the corner of Berkeley and Tremont streets.

Clarisse watched after him a moment and then turned onto Warren Avenue in front of the police station. She sidled between two parked cruisers, then ran across to her building. As she fished for the keys in her pocket she saw that the light was on in the back of Mr. Fred's Tease 'n' Tint. It gave an eerie illumination to the purple walls within. She walked over and peered inside, but saw no one inside.

She at last found her keys, held them up to the light from Mr. Fred's, and picked out the one to the front door. She then became aware of an odd scraping noise, somewhat like that of a foot being dragged through gravel, from somewhere above her. She looked up and squinted. Rain splashed into her eyes and blurred her vision. She wiped away the moisture with the back of her hand, and in that instant heard a *whoosh* as something square, black, heavy, and metallic smashed onto the sidewalk no more than six inches in back of her.

Clarisse froze, her heart hammering. She listened. She heard another scraping sound—like a step on gravel—above.

Then nothing.

She stared at the wreckage of the object behind her, and then cautiously looked up along the edges of the buildings. She saw nothing. She glanced down again and prodded the metallic wreckage with the toe of her shoe. Then she turned and walked swiftly across the street to the police station, keeping an eye over her shoulder.

In her wet fur, she quickly attracted the attention of one of the officers behind the desk. He came over, clicked open a ball-point pen, and slapped down a blank report sheet on the counter between them.

"Someone just tried to kill me with a video cassette recorder," Clarisse blurted.

The officer flicked his eyes up from the report sheet and looked her over. With his pen poised over a box halfway down the page, he asked, "VHS or Betamax?"

Part Three

Chapter Fifteen

A FEW MINUTES after eight o'clock on Christmas night, the screech of the casement of one of Clarisse's front windows being thrust up drew the attention of two policemen coming out of the quiet District D police station. A moment later the bottom of the Scotch pine was thrust through the opening. It wavered there a moment as if testing the air, and then the lower branches of the tree, temporarily caught by the window frame, were suddenly released as more of the tree was pushed out. The boughs of the pine were laden with glass ornaments, strings of lights, ropes of glass beads, and silver icicles. A number of the colored glass globes were shaken loose and dropped with little shattering explosions to the sidewalk below. The icicles fluttered in the frigid night air and caught the reflection of the station's blue neon light.

The two policemen watched with curiosity as the tree was eased farther and farther out of the window. At last, as the tree bent of its own weight and hung against the side of the building, they caught sight of two gloveless hands clutching the narrow top just below the lopsided silver star.

The hands suddenly let go of the tree, and it crashed—

decorated boughs, silver star, and all–to the sidewalk midway between the doors to Slate and the gutter. Clarisse poked her head out the window, and stared down at it with a satisfied smile. She then pulled back inside the window and slammed down the sash. This second screech, louder than the first, echoed eerily down deserted Warren Avenue.

Inside the apartment, Valentine sat comfortably sideways in an easy chair, his legs hooked over the arm, sipping his third bourbon and water of the evening.

Clarisse walked casually toward him, picking pine needles off her white blouse and gray wool slacks.

"Some people would at least wait until the day is officially ended before getting rid of the tree," Valentine remarked.

"I've been dying to get rid of that vision of Christmas Present ever since I walked in yesterday afternoon and found you decorating it."

"I shudder to think what you would have done if I'd erected a life-size crèche in here."

"No problem," said Clarisse, removing a final needle from her cuff. "I still have that acetylene torch in the closet." She grabbed the metal tree stand and then snatched up the small mound of wrapping paper and ribbon off the table and carried them into the kitchen. She came back a moment later with a scotch on the rocks. "The neighbors are going to start talking," she said, sitting back in the chair opposite Valentine. She reached out and edged the table lamp back a bit so that she could see him.

"About what?"

"Every time they look out the window, somebody's hurling something from an upper story onto the sidewalk. And usually it's being aimed straight for my head."

"You're lucky you weren't killed that time. Or maimed. Or scarred for life."

Clarisse gave him a tight smile. "Always the kind word. The gentle thought."

The police had been of no use in discovering who it was that had thrown the video cassette recorder from the roof. Two officers had accompanied her back across the street that night. In the rear of the building, they discovered the fire escape ladder pulled all the way down to the ground. They climbed to the roof, but found no sign that anyone had been lurking. The roof doors of both the buildings were firmly secured from inside. It wasn't that the police didn't believe her story–they had seen the crushed machine on the sidewalk–they just didn't have anything to go on. Clarisse had gone back to the station house and filled out some forms, which didn't have appropriate boxes for "Attempted Crushing," but when she went back home, she was startled to discover that the tangle of broken machine had been removed from the sidewalk. She then realized, too late, that its surface ought to have been dusted for fingerprints.

Valentine had questioned Linc again about what happened between him and Sweeney on the night of the murder, but Linc's story remained the same in every detail. Since Valentine and Clarisse had questioned him at Fritz, Linc had been sullen and silent. He came to Slate every day, did his work, supervised the work of the others under him, and went home at five. He didn't go up into the office unless he had to, and he never visited Valentine's apartment above. He seemed to avoid Clarisse altogether. Valentine thought this was on account of embarrassment and humiliation, but Clarisse felt that it might be something else.

Clarisse was spending most of her waking hours in the law library. The semester had ended before Christmas, which meant that papers, exams, and reports had had to be suffered through and handed in before the holiday. Valentine's time was devoted to tying up last-minute details for the opening of Slate. He dealt with liquor and soft-drink distributors; he set up schedules for the simultaneous shifts he and Ashes had agreed to work behind the bar; he arranged for Joe to work the door every night but Monday, the slowest bar night all over the city. And he designated work shifts for his newest hirelings, Felix and Larry, who would perform stock-running and pickup duties. At the same time he had to put together a separate crew to manage the bar during the day.

"The problem was," said Clarisse, "the cops didn't think that the attempt to murder me was deliberate. That is to say, they thought it was just an accident that a video cassette recorder was hurled at me off the top of a four-story building in the middle of a rainy night."

"We've been over this a dozen times," returned Valentine. "And we still can't figure out who in the world would want to kill you."

Clarisse sat up a bit. "A pretty desperate character with a bad aim."

"That," Valentine agreed, "or some psycho out to harm a fashionably dressed and defenseless woman. But let's not forget the gypsies. Those people hold vendettas. They were also pretty fond of dropping things off the roof in your general direction the night you evicted them."

Clarisse took a long swallow of her scotch. "No matter how you look at it, I'm a marked woman."

"Nothing's happened in three weeks," Valentine pointed out.

"But I still feel like I'm living under sentence of death," said Clarisse. "Maybe someone has been trying to do me in and I haven't noticed."

"I hardly think you'd miss a hail of bullets whizzing about your head, or butcher knives thwacking into the wall behind you. And what if whoever it was wasn't trying to kill you? What if it was only a warning to stop snooping around about Sweeney Drysdale?"

"I would have preferred an anonymous telephone call or one of those messages with the letters cut out of magazines." She took another sip of her drink and then said in a brave, resigned voice, "No, I'm a marked woman, Val."

"Oh, brother . . ." Valentine groaned softly.

"Will you still be so heartless when you have to go to the

Southern Mortuary to identify my battered, barely recognizable remains?"

Valentine shrugged nonchalantly, drained his glass, and set it on the table. "I think what you should do and what I should do is stop talking about this."

"Fine," Clarisse said. "As long as we start *doing* something about it." She looked at him with a steady eye. "Agreed?"

Valentine considered. "All right. I suppose. But tomorrow. Tonight I think we ought to do something to mark this holiday. We can't have people saying we're not traditionalists."

"I already threw the tree out the window. I lied to my family, telling them I was in Barbados for two weeks with someone whose last name was DuPont so that I could spend the holiday with you. What more do you want?"

"To do the same thing we did last Christmas night."

Clarisse leaned over her chair and grabbed the *Globe* from the carpet. She scanned the entertainment pages and then looked up at Valentine over the edge of the paper. "It's either *Cinderella* at the Beacon Hill, or *Dr. Butcher—Medical Deviant* at the Palace."

Valentine thought a moment. "The Disney film," he said. "I prefer my sadism animated this evening."

———

———

CINDERELLA proved as delightful as they had remembered it. When they emerged into Government Center at eleven-thirty, the clock tower of Park Street Church marked the time with a single chime.

"We still have half an hour of this festive day left," Clarisse said, "and the Last Hurrah is only about fifty paces away."

"I know a better bar," said Valentine. "One you actually haven't been drunk in yet."

Clarisse ignored his remark and walked with him across the street to hail a cab in front of the Parker House. "Where are we going? I hate surprises—especially on holidays."

Wordlessly, Valentine opened the back door of a taxi parked beneath the hotel marquee and Clarisse climbed inside. Before he got in behind her, Valentine gave the address to the driver in a low voice that Clarisse could not make out.

———

———

TEN minutes later, seated on a barstool, Clarisse said, "You were right. I have never been drunk here before."

Smiling with proprietary pride, Valentine stood behind Slate's bar. Fresh drinks stood between them. A single glass ball, rescued from the wreck of the Scotch pine just outside the door, dangled from a hook over the mirror. Valentine had lighted candles rather than turning on the overhead lights. A new tape slowly revolved on the tape deck, and soft rock music filled the corners.

"Nice place you got here," she said.

"I like it," Valentine said, raising his glass in a toast. "Here's to bleary days ahead."

Clarisse raised her glass and saluted him: "Here's to prosperity and success in our chosen endeavors."

She glanced around, peering into the obscurity. "It *looks* all ready."

"By candlelight, sure . . ."

There was a lull in the conversation, and after a moment Clarisse said, "I was serious about what I said earlier—about trying to find out why a dead gossip columnist ended up in my bed. We could try a little fancy footwork and see what we could come up with."

Valentine smiled. "I'll dust off my tap shoes tonight, but I think it may be a bigger production number than we anticipate right now."

Clarisse finished her drink and set the glass aside. "That's all right," she said. "My adrenalin's still up after a whole semester of school."

"Where to start?" said Valentine. "That's the problem."

"We'll figure that out tomorrow." Clarisse eased off her stool. "Tonight I just want to settle down for a long winter's nap."

"And I'm going to wander over to the Eagle and pick up one last Christmas present for myself."

"A GI Joe," Clarisse asked, "or a Nutcracker?"

———

———

CLIMBING to the second floor, Clarisse was engulfed by the noise of a television turned to highest volume from Julia and Susie's apartment. She sighed and rapped her knuckles on their apartment door but got no response. She lifted her foot and slammed the side of her heel once with as much force as she could muster against the bottom of the door. The door rattled loudly.

The noise ceased abruptly, and the door opened.

Julia, wearing a white T-shirt and men's army fatigues with bright red socks pulled up over the cuffs, stood with an empty punch glass in one hand.

"Come on in," she said by way of greeting, "I'm lonesome and they're just about to show *A Christmas Carol.*"

Clarisse was going to refuse, but the melancholy flickering about Julia's eyes stopped her. "Just for a while," she said, and followed the woman inside. It was the first time Clarisse had been in the apartment in more than a month. On the television Scrooge was silently berating Bob Cratchitt.

"Where's Susie?"

"On a date," said Julia bitterly.

"Tonight?"

"Money talks," replied Julia morosely. "And money dances, and Susie's always needing a partner, even on Christmas. Have some eggnog? I made it myself. I was just going to have some more."

Clarisse nodded agreement and Julia went into the kitchen. She soon came out with another punch glass and her own filled. The top of each was covered with a swirl of nutmeg.

Julia plopped onto one end of the sofa and Clarisse sat at the other. Clarisse looked at the television screen as Scrooge was horrified by the specter of Marley's ghost appearing on his door knocker.

"I didn't think you watched anything but sports," Clarisse said idly, and in that moment, she noticed that the video cassette recorder was missing from its space on the shelf below the television set. "What happened to your recorder?" Clarisse asked in a choked voice.

"It got broken," Julia said flatly, looking over at her.

"Oh?" Clarisse said casually. "When?"

"The other day," said Julia vaguely. "What's the matter? You don't like my eggnog? Merry Christmas. Drink up."

Clarisse stared at the contents of the punch glass.

Julia laughed. "You act like it's arsenic in there instead of bourbon and cream."

Chapter Sixteen

AT A QUARTER to eleven the following morning, Clarisse opened her apartment door to admit Miss America. The young woman carried her manicure tray around her hunched shoulders. She shivered violently.

"It's freezing, freezing, freezing," said Miss America. "This is how cold it gets on Mount Rainier."

Clarisse removed the coat loosely draped over Miss America's frail form. Above one breast on her starched green uniform, Miss America had pinned a redwood brooch in the shape of California. Rhinestones marked Los Angeles and San Francisco.

"Would you like coffee, America?" Clarisse offered. "I just made a fresh pot."

"No, but thanks. I don't mean to rush you or anything, but I really am squeezing you in. We're booked solid for the rest of the week—what with New Year's and all. I'll bet you're pretty busy over here too. I've got seventeen Spuds coming in on Thursday and Friday."

"Spuds?" echoed Clarisse vaguely.

"Long Island Spuds," Miss America said by way of explanation, and looked around the room. Still mystified, Clarisse
indicated the chair they would use, and then went toward the kitchen. Miss America knelt before the chair, and spread out a thin
yard-square sheet of opaque pink plastic on the carpet. "They're a
motorcycle club. I don't know why they'd want to name a motorcycle club after a potato, though. Anyway, I'm going to tell them
to be sure to come to the opening of Slate."

"We'd appreciate that. You and Mr. Fred have a lot of clout in
certain segments of the community."

"Thank you," said Miss America modestly.

"I can't tell you how much I appreciate your dropping
everything to do this for me," Clarisse called from the kitchen.
"I've been running late all morning, and I have this interview at
twelve. I just forgot to make an appointment before you and Mr.
Fred went to your mother's for the weekend. Did you have a nice
Christmas?"

"Fred gave me a doorstop made out of petrified wood," said
Miss America. "It was exactly what I've always wanted.
Somebody must have told him."

Clarisse came back into the living room with a cup of steaming black coffee. She found Miss America kneeling on the carpet
at the edge of the plastic, her clips, files, buffs, brushes, bowls,
and liquids spread out neatly before her. "I'm sorry," she apologized, "but Fred makes me charge double for emergency out-
calls."

"It'll be worth every penny, America."

Clarisse settled into the chair, and America asked her to cross
one leg over the other. When Clarisse had done so, America gently removed the red slipper from that foot. She set the slipper aside
and studied Clarisse's foot a moment, turning it this way and that
in the pale winter morning light.

"You have beautiful feet," said America, as a connoisseur.
"Beautiful feet are inherited, you know. Just like noses. And
earlobes. Are these your mother's feet or your father's?"

"The toes are my father's," said Clarisse. "The arch is my mother's."

Miss America chose a file and began work, starting with the largest toe of that foot. "Most people's feet won't stand up to inspection," said Miss America severely. "You come across this gorgeous woman—beautiful hair, beautiful nose, been everywhere, done everything, fifteen offers of marriage a month—and then you look at her feet, and you wonder what all the excitement's about. It's no wonder so many people wear shoes." America glanced up. "Why do you need a pedicure to go on an interview? What kind of interview is it, anyway?"

"It's for law school. A kind of special assignment," Clarisse replied mysteriously. "And I wanted to wear a pair of open-toed shoes I bought last week."

"It's fifteen degrees below zero outside," said Miss America, pointing with a file at the thick frost on the windowpanes.

"I know," sighed Clarisse. "I had no idea, when I started this career, that I would become not only a lawyer, but a slave to fashion."

"Fashion can be a trap," agreed Miss America. "I see its victims every day. Some women don't think about anything else except their eyes, their hair, their nails, their feet, what clothes they wear, who they know, what other people say about them, where they get invited to, who their boyfriends are, and how much money they make. It's really terrible."

"I know," said Clarisse, sipping her coffee. "You're lucky to have an interest in national parks. That's very educational. That's worth spending time on."

"I dream about them," said America confidingly. "I really do. I mean, last night I dreamed about Old Faithful. Every year for my birthday Fred gives me a trip to a national park. This spring I'm going back to Yellowstone."

"I've never been there," said Clarisse. "Do you have pictures from your last trip?"

"I don't take pictures. I just buy postcards."

"Really? I'd think you'd want something more personal."

"No," said America, buffing. "Fred gave me a camera, but I kept putting my finger over the lens. Besides, I don't like things hanging around my neck." She indicated the tray. "I get enough of that in the shop. Also, I like the colors on postcards better. They're more like real life."

"You should look into getting a video setup. Then you could make live-action tapes of Old Faithful–and the bears, and all that."

"I've thought of that," said America, "but video equipment is very expensive."

"Susie and Julia love theirs."

"I don't think they have a camera, just a player and a recorder," said America.

Clarisse drained half her cup of coffee. "Valentine and I have been thinking of getting a video recorder. That way he can tape 'All My Children' and 'Ryan's Hope' for me when I'm at school or studying."

"Do you watch 'All My Children'?" asked America. "Fred and I do, too. Whenever we don't have customers at one o'clock. Fred wants to rename the shop Opal's Glamorama in honor of Opal Gardner, but who'd take a name like that seriously? I told him he'd better stick with Mr. Fred's T 'n' T."

"I wonder which is better," mused Clarisse, "VHS or Betamax."

"One of them is better," said America vaguely. "I don't know which, though. You should ask Susie and Julia."

"What kind do they have?"

"Betamax."

"Are you sure?" Clarisse asked, a bit too eagerly.

"It's *all* Susie talked about when they first bought it," said America with mock weariness. "Every time she'd come in the shop she'd go on and on about their new Betamax and what she'd recorded on it and how much more sex she and Julia were having now that they had it. I never figured out that part. I think they ought to read a book once in a while. Last Christmas I gave them a big picture book on Carlsbad Caverns, but I don't think they even looked at the pictures." America shook her head, and concluded, "I don't know . . ."

Clarisse did not reply, but at a touch from America's hand, she switched feet. Then for a few moments she stared out the window at the slash of late-morning gray sky above the police station.

Clarisse took a sip from her mug, put it down again, and stared at the top of America's head.

"America," she said, "you remember that party you gave for Valentine and me?"

"Of course," said America, "that was the night Sweeney got killed."

"Right. Why do you think he crashed that party?"

"Sweeney? Sweeney didn't crash that party. He was invited. Fred invited him."

"Really? Mr. Fred and Sweeney were friends?"

Miss America looked up curiously. "Sweeney and Fred used to be lovers," she said. The expression on Clarisse's face must have been one of shock, for America laughed. "I thought you knew. *Everybody* knew that."

"Valentine and I didn't."

"Sure. Sweeney was working as a bartender down at the Hungry Eye in those days and Fred was in a cut-rate salon over on Kneeland Street in Chinatown. This was when Mr. Fred was out on his own, you know, and didn't have me to help him. I would never have let him work cut-rate. It was my idea he should have the T 'n' T and I helped him raise the money and everything. Anyway, Fred used to go over to the Hungry Eye for a few drinks after work and that's how they met."

"Well, that was nice," said Clarisse politely.

"Except it wasn't nice at all," said America, and her touch on

Clarisse's foot tightened, "because Fred used to go over there for breakfast and lunch—and even coffee breaks. Fred was this terrible lush—I mean really terrible—and finally Sweeney stopped serving him and made him go to AA and all that. It's the best thing anybody ever did for Fred. I guess it kind of made an impression on him when a *bartender* told him to go to AA, and of course Fred had this huge crush on Sweeney. A lot of people seem to get crushes on bartenders at one time or another."

"Yes," said Clarisse curtly.

"Anyway," Miss America went on, "they lived together for a few months and then they broke up. That was sort of nasty, but then they got to be friends again, and Sweeney was always putting something nice in the column about us. I mean, a lot of people didn't like him, but Mr. Fred and I sure did. Or at least we liked him most of the time."

"What do you mean?"

"I mean that Sweeney was one of those people who'd pat you on the back with one hand while he was cutting your throat with the other."

"Are you talking about something specific that happened?"

"No," said Miss America. "I just mean that I liked Sweeney, but I didn't trust him. Mr. Fred did, though. He was very upset when Sweeney got killed. He said Sweeney was the first person he had ever gone to bed with that died. He said it was a terrible feeling."

"I can imagine," said Clarisse sympathetically. "I'm a little surprised, though, that Mr. Fred would invite Sweeney to a party when he knew that Julia and Susie were going to be there."

"I know," agreed Miss America. "I told him he probably shouldn't, but Fred likes fireworks. Fred's favorite holiday is the Fourth of July. Now, what color is your dress?"

"My dress?"

"I have to know what color to paint your nails," said Miss

America patiently. "What color dress are you wearing to the interview?"

"Canary," said Clarisse.

———

———

"IS this Captain Video? I'm calling to find out if the VCR Julia Logan dropped off for repairs last week is ready yet." Valentine moved the receiver from one ear to the other. "Sure, I'll hold."

He lodged the receiver in the crook of his shoulder as he leaned back in his chair. He pulled his feet up onto the corner of his desk and crossed them at the ankles. As he waited for the repair service to come back on the line he tapped the nub of his pen against the open Yellow Pages. Bold blue lines had been drawn through the names, addresses, and numbers of forty-four video supply and repair shops listed in the greater Boston area.

He stretched his neck, and heard the bones crack. He knew there were persons who made a living on the telephone, but after an hour and twenty minutes of it, he wondered how they did it. His ears hurt from having the receiver jammed against them for so long.

With a click, Captain Video came back on the line.

"I see," said Valentine after a moment. "Maybe she left it off under the name Susie Whitebread," said Valentine cautiously.

The line went on hold again. Some of them hung up when he asked them to check under "Whitebread."

Valentine swiveled the chair slightly so that he could look through the one-way mirror into the bar. The day before, in a junk shop around the corner on Tremont Street, he'd found an old telephone booth with an accordion door and insets of blue-tinted glass in the sides. He had picked it up for a couple of hundred dollars and sent Linc's assistants over to fetch it. They were putting it in place now, between the doors of the two rest rooms. At the end of the bar, Ashes sat drinking from a can of caffeine-free Coke while going over a stack of notes, trying to put together his Ashes Flashes column for the week.

"Not under Whitebread either?" said Valentine. "Sorry to have bothered you. I'm sure this was the shop she told me to call. Thanks anyway."

Valentine hung up and struck a blue line across the name and address and number of the shop. He tossed the pen aside and dragged his feet off the desk. He stood up to stretch and groaned. He looked through the window and watched as Linc and a helper carefully cut a rectangle of space from the back of the overturned booth.

Clarisse knocked and entered from the hallway.

"Any luck?" she asked, as she removed her fur hat and dropped it into a chair. She shook her hair loose and then removed her coat as well. Her expression was weary, but her face was brightly flushed with cold.

"Four more shops to call," said Valentine, checking the directory. "Video Villa, Video Visuals, Videosphere Productions, and Wholesome Film Center Incorporated." He tugged at his earlobes, and grimaced. "I struck out forty-five times. How about you?"

"Nothing. I went to all the repair shops in the South End, and none of them had ever heard of Susie or Julia. Actually, some of them had heard of Susie, but they were sure that she hadn't brought in a VCR to be repaired. My feet are frozen."

"But well-groomed."

Clarisse threw herself into the desk chair, looked in the directory, and punched out the number of Video Villa.

Valentine went downstairs briefly to watch the telephone booth being upended into place. He complimented Linc on his work, read over Ashes' column, and then returned to the office.

"That's that," said Clarisse. "No shop did business with them.

And what do we have for our trouble? Frostbitten toes for me. Cauliflower ears for you."

"We have a little more than that," said Valentine. "We know that somebody tried to kill you with a Betamax, and we know that Julia and Susie's Betamax is missing. Julia told you it was being repaired, but we know that it's not at any repair shop in the Boston area."

"That kind of negative proof is inadmissible," said Clarisse.

"You know the problem with all this?" said Valentine.

"What?"

"Nobody has a sufficient motive. Nothing to risk killing for. Julia and Susie–blackmail that happened five years ago? Come on. And Julia already had her revenge on Sweeney–she broke his arm, remember? Ashes wants a two-bit column in a two-bit throwaway rag? That's hardly the top of the publishing heap. And Mr. Fred, still upset about some lovers' tiff that happened five or six years ago when he was a lush? And Linc–no motive at all." Valentine paused for a beat, and then said, "You know what I think the missing piece of the puzzle is?"

"What?"

"That last column Sweeney wrote. The one Ashes said got lost. The one Joe saw on Ashes' desk."

Clarisse looked at him, but said nothing.

Chapter Seventeen

VALENTINE and Clarisse had made no progress in their investigation into the murder of Sweeney Drysdale II. The following four days were taken up with the last-minute details for the opening of Slate. On Saturday evening, at nine o'clock, all the months of hard work began to pay off. The doors opened and the celebration began. A line of men, three and four abreast, snaked along Warren Avenue and around the corner by the abandoned playground. The night was cold, though not as frigid as it had been on Christmas. There was no wind, however, and no one complained.

Inside, Valentine and Ashes were kept continually busy behind the bar. Valentine wore a tuxedo shirt with a black bow tie and black leather pants. Ashes wore the same outfit except for the addition of a black leather vest. The newly hired runners, Felix and Larry, were in constant motion bringing supplies from the cellar and making sure bottles of beer and drink glasses did not clutter the wall shelves and dark corners. Clarisse came down about nine-thirty and edged onto a stool between Valentine and Ashes' stations. Valentine mixed a scotch and water for her. She

wore a full length gown of dove-gray watered silk; a small cluster
of white camellias rested in the gathered V of the bodice. They
had been sent, along with a congratulatory telegram, from Noah
Lovelace. He had decided, after all, not to attend the opening of
the bar. Clarisse's hair was swept gracefully back from her face
and in each earlobe was a tiny silver star. She swiveled about on
her stool with her drink in hand and looked about. The barroom
was pleasantly crowded and the air was sparked with laughter and
conversation beneath the loud music.

The patterned tin ceiling was completely obscured by a mass
of black and white balloons and packets of silver confetti. The thin
silver netting holding the decorations was to be released precisely
on the twelfth stroke of midnight. Multicolored streamers dangled
to a point just above the patrons' heads and were kept in constant
gentle motion by slowly revolving ceiling fans. Two pale amber
beams played constantly across the crowd and the slate walls were
blushed with patches of red and pink light. Clarisse turned back to
the bar and was about to try to get Valentine's attention when she
noticed Linc at the end stool at the front of the bar. He sat hunched
forward, staring at Valentine as he guzzled a beer. From his expression, Clarisse wondered if he were practicing some speech
that he hoped would bring him back into Valentine's graces–and
bed–by midnight.

Finally she captured Valentine's attention and he came over,
in high spirits.

"You're stunning," he said. "And this evening is well on its
way to becoming the best in my life."

"The whole world looks beautiful to you this evening," she
added, "at least as much of it as you can see within this barroom."

"Did you see Mr. Fred and Miss America?" He nodded
toward the back, and Clarisse had to sit up slightly for a clear
view. Mr. Fred and his sister stood among a small knot of leather-
clad, bearded men–the Long Island Spuds, Clarisse supposed.
Fred wore a tuxedo completely covered with deep scarlet

spangles, the intense color relieved only by black piping along the wide lapels and the pockets. America's hair was fixed into a loose chignon encircling the back of her head. She wore a white forties-style dress with padded shoulders, dark hose, and ankle-strap heels. In one hand she held a white clutch bag and with the other she turned the wrist of the tallest of the Spuds, critically examining his nails. Mr. Fred was chatting amiably with three more of them, and taking tiny sips from a can of Tab.

"America looks great," Clarisse remarked, "but where in the civilized world did Mr. Fred get that outfit?"

"America made it for him."

Clarisse turned and nodded once in the opposite direction, toward Linc. "Is he trying for a New Year's reconciliation?"

"He's building up to it, but every time he looks like he's about to have meaningful conversation I slide another beer across to him."

"Come midnight, he'll be crying in those beers."

Valentine shrugged. "The room is full of shoulders more than willing to bear Linc's tears."

A number of men were leaning over the bar trying to capture Valentine's attention. He winked at Clarisse and went back to work. Clarisse took a long swallow of her scotch and turned toward the bar's main entrance. Apologetic Joe was sitting on a stool to the right of the door, checking the ID's of those who appeared under age. Putting down her glass and easing off the stool, Clarisse made her way over to him.

"How's it going, Joe?" she asked.

He handed back a photo identification card to a young man and then glanced at the counter in his other hand. He depressed a button and the line of numbers increased by one. "We're already over capacity. That's great."

"Joe, I left my keys up in my apartment and I need to go up to the office. Can I borrow yours?"

Joe checked another ID, clicked his counter again, and then

reached around and unhooked his key ring from a back belt loop.

Clarisse took the entire ring and then stepped quickly away. She edged through the coat check room and went up the circular staircase. The office door was already unlocked and Clarisse hurried inside. She didn't turn on the light, but grabbed her fur coat from the coat rack where she'd left it earlier that day. She went out onto the landing and closed the office door behind her. She was startled by Julia and Susie's voices, coming down the stairs from the landing above.

"Will you move it, woman?" Susie demanded. "It's already eleven o'clock and we have got less less'n an hour to get feelin' good. Now come on, come on, move it!"

"Douse your jets, bitch, I'm hurryin'!" Julia shot back, but there was no anger in her voice.

Clarisse met the two women on the landing.

"Where you goin'?" demanded Julia.

"Party that bad, huh?" said Susie.

"The party's great," returned Clarisse, "but Valentine needs another hundred pounds of ice, and I said I'd get it for him. Here," she said, unlocking the door to the office, "you two go through here. That way you won't have to wait in line outside."

"Whoa, thanks!" said Susie, and preceded Julia into the office. After Clarisse had shut the door behind them, and checked to make sure it locked, she descended to the street. She held her coat closed and excused herself through the line of waiting men. She commandeered a taxi that had just deposited four lethally drunk men in front of the bar.

Through the partition window she gave the driver her destination, and then sat back and relaxed for the short drive. Now and then she glanced out the window at knots of revelers on the sidewalk and occasionally in the street itself. Every restaurant and bar they drove past was crowded and noisy. Even though windows had been shut against the cold, the sound of partying could be heard from almost every apartment building.

When the taxi came to a stop before a townhouse on upper Marlborough Street, Clarisse asked the driver to wait, but he refused. She paid him, leaving a pointedly small tip, and climbed out of the taxi. She rushed across the sidewalk and up the steps of the building.

After searching for the correct key from Joe's ring to unlock the door, Clarisse went inside. She was hit with the noise of loud music and a maze of voices crashing down from the upper floors.

Clarisse had never been to Paul Ashe's apartment before, but she had remembered the address from some paperwork that she had helped Valentine with only the day before. She knew from off-handed remarks from Ashes that he lived in a basement flat, and she hoped that she wouldn't have to choose between doors. She hurried across the small entrance area, picked up the hem of her dress, and descended a narrow flight of uncarpeted stairs to the single apartment door at the basement level. Nailed to the door was a triangular metal road sign reading Dangerous Equipment Ahead.

Now she only had to hope that Ashes had given Apologetic Joe a key to his place, and that Joe kept the key on the ring that Clarisse held in her nervous hand. The tension in her face eased for a moment as the third key she tried turned the bolt in the lock. She opened the door and stepped over the threshold, easing the door shut behind her. She stood in the dark a moment, just listening.

She heard nothing but the hum of the refrigerator, and the traffic outside on Marlborough Street.

She slid the palm of her hand up along the wall by the side of the door and found the switch. The ceiling light in the living room came on blindingly, and at the same time the stereo receiver began blasting out the Stompers' new hit single at full volume.

Clarisse slapped at the wall switch and the room was again plunged into darkness and silence.

She bumped her way across the room and turned on a floor

lamp she had seen in the instant of light and noise. Clarisse hadn't
known what to expect to find in Ashes' apartment—three rooms
with a dungeon motif, perhaps. It looked, however, as if most of
the furniture had come from a family beach house. The larger
pieces were of natural-color wicker with chintz-covered cushions.
A pale-blue-and-tan Oriental carpet covered the floor. Two of the
living room walls were floor-to-ceiling bookcases, and all the
shelves were full to overflowing. On the coffee table Joe's
Walkman rested on the open pages of the current *Rolling Stone*. A
doorway to Clarisse's right opened into a narrow walk-in kitchen,
and another doorway in the back led to a bedroom that looked to
be substantially larger than the living room.

Clarisse crossed to Ashes' desk and seated herself in a
Hitchcock chair. She immediately began searching through all the
drawers, carefully attempting to return anything she removed to
its original position. Sweeney Drysdale's missing column was not
to be found. She stood and moved about the room, looking in
every corner, on every shelf, and under and around every piece of
furniture that might make a good hiding place. She decided to
assume that Ashes had not hidden the column in any of his books,
because that would have been too obvious—and because it would
have been impossible to look through them all, anyway.

She went into the kitchen and pulled on the chain light. On a
shelf above the old-fashioned gas stove, between a can marked
Coffee and a can marked Tea, she saw a neatly folded sheet of
white typing paper. Clarisse smiled, took down the sheet, and
carefully unfolded it.

She found three typewritten recipes for Italian casseroles.

Suppressing the intense desire to crumple it up in frustration,
she refolded the page and put it back on the shelf.

She went through the utensil drawer, plundered the cabinets
above and beneath the sink, peered along the shelves of the
refrigerator, and rolled out the vegetable crispers. She pulled out
the light and returned to the living room. She went into the

bedroom and snapped on a dark blue ginger-jar lamp on the nightstand. She seated herself on the edge of the unmade bed and looked around. The brick-walled bedroom was dark and cluttered; there was track lighting, and Christmas tree lights were webbed against the wall facing the bed. More books were stacked against the wall. The open doors of the louvered closet revealed a long rack of clothes on hangers, and on the floor of the closet a tangle of discarded jeans, flannel shirts, and black engineer boots. On a shelf on top were half a dozen large clear-plastic boxes filled with ropes, buckles, black leather straps, underwear, and things she couldn't quite imagine a use for. In the corner, its base weighted with stacks of glossy magazines, was a four-foot Christmas tree, complete with twinkling white lights, silver balls, tinsel, and, on the top, a silver angel playing a tiny silver violin.

The bedroom was so cluttered Clarisse didn't know where to begin to look for the column. She glanced at the bedside table. Beside an amber glass ashtray littered with several varieties of cigarette butts was an open pack of Kools.

Clarisse wanted one desperately.

She opened the drawer of the bedside table. Inside were just the sorts of things that Valentine kept in his bedside table. She picked about in there for a moment, and then looked longingly at the cigarettes again.

She pushed the Kools a little farther away. The pack fell to the floor between the table and the bed. Moving the table in order to reach it, she suddenly saw her face reflected in a silver glass ball that had evidently fallen from the tree and rolled across the floor. She smiled down at her reflected image in the distorting surface of the silver ball. She saw the light bulb in the ginger-jar lamp – and she saw something else as well.

She slid her hand up under the nightstand, and found a business-size envelope taped to the bottom of the drawer. With growing excitement she carefully peeled the envelope free. She held it in her hand a moment before employing a long thumbnail to slit open the sealed flap. She pulled two typewritten sheets of paper out and smoothed them open across her thigh.

In the upper left hand corner of the first page was typed:

Sweeney Drysdale II

Column

BAR, Issue 82, Vol. III

She read the items quickly, discounting them one by one. Her foot tapped in anxiety. At the last lines on the second page, her foot stopped in the midst of a downward beat.

She reread the item, folded the sheets of paper closed again, then slipped them back into the envelope and put it into her left coat pocket. She picked up the cigarette package that had fallen, put the bedside table back in its place, and snapped out the lamp. Unceremoniously she let herself out of the apartment, then rushed up the steps and flew across the entryway to the front door.

She had no difficulty in securing another taxi.

Chapter Eighteen

CLARISSE shoved through the doors of Slate at only twenty minutes before midnight. One of the panels slammed into Joe's knee where he sat in the entranceway.

"Sorry, Clarisse," said Joe. "I guess I was too close."

"It's all right," said Clarisse hurriedly, gazing across the enormous crowd. In the last half hour, Joe had admitted everyone in line. Fire inspectors went into hibernation on New Year's Eve, and Slate, like every bar in town, was crowded far past its legal capacity. Joe touched Clarisse's sleeve. "I thought you were up in the office," he said.

"I got called away suddenly," she said. "I had to go to a sick friend's apartment."

"I hope they're better," said Joe earnestly. "Have you got my keys? I feel naked sitting here without them."

Clarisse reached impatiently into her coat pocket and dropped the key ring into Joe's waiting palm.

"Thanks," said Joe. "And Happy New Year."

"It had better be," said Clarisse darkly.

Clarisse pushed through to the bar, offering few apologies on the way. Holding plastic champagne glasses, Mr. Fred, Miss America, and Julia were crowded at Ashes' end of the bar. Mr. Fred's glass was filled with what Clarisse hoped was a soft drink. Julia was dressed in black tie and tails, with her leather motorcycle hat raked back on her head.

Clarisse slipped between Miss America and Julia. Ashes stood facing her, filling a dozen or so of the glasses with champagne. Several dozen more were neatly lined up nearby. Clarisse held her hand over the next glass he was to fill.

"You don't want any?" he asked.

"I want Valentine," said Clarisse. "Tell him to come down here."

"Clarisse, we're very busy," Ashes complained.

Clarisse grabbed the bottle from his hand. *"Now,"* she said.

Miss America, Mr. Fred, and Julia glanced uncomfortably at one another. Ashes headed down to the other end of the bar. Clarisse began filling glasses herself while she waited.

Down at the other end, Ashes tapped Valentine on the shoulder and then conferred with him briefly. Linc, still sitting where he had been all evening, peered past Valentine at Clarisse. His glance was worried.

"Is anything wrong?" asked Miss America, gently touching Clarisse's arm.

"I'm fine," said Clarisse grimly, continuing to pour.

In an attempt to lighten the tone, Mr. Fred exclaimed, "Don't you love my jacket, Clarisse? America made it especially for tonight. The fittings were *hell*. She stuck so many pins in me I felt like a voodoo doll."

"It's gorgeous, Mr. Fred," said Clarisse perfunctorily. She looked at Julia as she put down the empty bottle. "Where's Susie?"

"Over in the corner," Julia said sourly, "talking to a couple of her regulars."

"Regulars? In here?"

"Vice cops from across the street."

At that moment, Susie Whitebread came up behind Julia. She wore matching black tie, and her hair had been permed into a short afro. "You're my only vice," she said, snaking her arm around Julia's waist. At that moment Ashes and Valentine appeared. As Clarisse was about to speak to them, Susie exclaimed, "And wasn't no cop I was talking to neither! I was talking to Ashes' friend who fixed our Betamax." She smiled at the bartender. "He did a fan-fuck-ing-tas-tic job on that piece of machinery, honey. I thought I was never gonna get to look at Miss Nav-ra-ti-lov-a again!"

Valentine's eyes widened when he heard this, and he glanced at Clarisse. She looked back without apparent surprise.

"Repair shops rip you off," said Ashes. "Glad he was able to help you, Susie."

Linc had threaded his way through the crowd and now stood just behind Clarisse, sipping his beer and trying to pretend that he had come there only by chance.

Valentine stood uneasily behind the bar, looking back to his deserted station. All the champagne glasses were gone, and about three dozen men down there were clamoring for more. "What's this all about, Clarisse?" he asked impatiently.

Clarisse whipped the open envelope from her pocket, and withdrew the two folded sheets of paper. She shook them open and held them up for Valentine to see. She dropped them face up on the bar.

"Now we go upstairs," she said, looking at Valentine and Ashes.

Julia, Susie, Mr. Fred, Miss America, Linc, and a drunk that nobody had ever seen before craned around to try to get a look at the papers.

"How in the hell did you get hold of *that*?" demanded Ashes incredulously. He made a grab for them, but Clarisse smoothly slid them out of the reach of his grasp.

"What is it?" cried Mr. Fred excitedly. "America, can you see what it is?"

"No," said Miss America, who had been standing right next to the pages. She backed away from the bar. Julia sidled in closer and glanced at the papers on the bar. She craned her neck to get a better look. She turned back to Susie and said, "Somebody better turn off them fans up there, or we are *all* gonna get splattered."

"You bet," Clarisse snapped without taking her eyes from Ashes.

Linc began to edge away into the crowd again, but Clarisse, who caught this movement, reached around and clutched his biceps. "Stay," she said with brittle sweetness. "Hang around for a while."

Valentine signaled to Felix and told him to get Larry and come behind the bar to continue filling champagne glasses. "We'll be back in a few minutes," he assured the nervous runner.

"Can America and I come, too?" Mr. Fred asked Clarisse as he looked about for his sister. He couldn't see her in the crush.

Clarisse gathered up the papers. "No," she said, somewhat coldly. She turned to him and stared for a moment into his cherubic face. "You know, Mr. Fred, I think you may be in a little trouble. And I'm not sure if America is going to be able to get you out of it this time."

"What?" said Mr. Fred, his smile disappearing suddenly. "What are you talking about, Clarisse?"

"Don't leave, Mr. Fred," she said. "We're going to want to speak to you in a little while."

Clarisse pushed Linc toward the coat check room. Valentine and Ashes came from behind the bar and followed them up to the office.

———

———

CLARISSE sat stiffly in one of the armchairs. Linc had seated himself nervously and uncertainly on the edge of the other. Valentine perched on the edge of the desk while Ashes, with folded arms, leaned back against the one-way mirror, glaring at Clarisse.

She handed Valentine the two sheets of paper, and he began reading. Ashes turned and stared down into the massive crowd in the bar below. The clock read twelve minutes of twelve.

"The good part is at the bottom of the second page," said Clarisse.

Valentine flipped over the page, and read aloud: *" 'Men, do you need your 'stashe put in shape? Ladies, would you like a shellacked dip that reaches into the next room? Well, run, drive, or fly to your neighborhood drug box — called an automatic bank teller in some circles — and then keep on going to a dynamite little spot where you will not only be dealt with fairly, but can get a splendid tease, a terrific tint, a perfect perm, and a dynamic dye — to say nothing of gladness by the gram, ecstasy by the ounce, and complete contentment by the capsule. Where, you ask, is this truly special haven of tonsorial splendor and chemical happiness? It's been a well-kept secret for years, but if you can fill in the blanks below, you can get your hair curled and your brain fried at the same time. Got a pencil? Try it, guys and girls. It's Mr. F***'s T**** 'n' T***, down on W*rr*n Ave***, across from D*str**t D, and right next door to the soon-to-be S*ate.' "*

Valentine looked up and around. "Mr. Fred *deals*? Mr. *Fred*?"

"It's not as bad as Sweeney made out," Ashes replied calmly. "Nothing heavy — mostly just ups and downs. He does it more as a convenience for his girls than anything else." He looked at Valentine and Clarisse. "Sweeney always knew about it."

"Then why did he suddenly decide to print it?" Valentine asked.

"Miss America said —" Ashes began.

"America knows about this column?" Clarisse exclaimed.

"Sure. I showed it to her the day after I found it in Sweeney's desk," said Ashes. "It seems that one of Fred's clients had been making house calls on a mayoral candidate — while his wife was in the house. Sweeney found out about it and thought it was hot enought to peddle to the press, which it probably was. He wanted Fred to pump the hooker for all the sordid info he could get on the candidate. Fred refused, and Sweeney got angry and yelled a lot, but Fred wouldn't back down."

"So Sweeney threatened to put that item in the column if Fred wouldn't change his mind," said Valentine.

"Sweeney told him he was going to shut down the Tease 'n' Tint," said Ashes flatly.

"So that's what he meant," murmured Linc, then snapped his mouth shut.

They all looked at him, and after a moment's consideration, Linc relented. "When I was telling Sweeney all about Rent-a-Wrench, he said he knew of this great space that was going to be opening up soon, and it was very close by. He said it would be perfect for me and he could pull strings and make sure I got it. Obviously, he was talking about Mr. Fred's place."

"What strings could he have pulled?" Valentine asked. "Linc, you know Clarisse and I control that building."

Clarisse sat forward in her chair. "Why did you lie about not being able to find the column?" she asked Ashes.

Ashes hesitated. He glanced again down to the bar, and then said lightly, "Oh, you never know when evidence like that might come in handy."

"For blackmail?" asked Valentine.

Ashes impassively raised his brows, but made no denial.

"Why did you show the column to America?" Clarisse wanted to know. "Why do you care what happens to Fred?"

"I'm his supplier," said Ashes bluntly.

"Did Sweeney know that?" asked Valentine quickly.

Ashes nodded toward the column. "Obviously he didn't. He'd have had blood in his mouth if he had known."

They were all silent a moment, then Linc blurted out, "What am I doing here? I didn't have anything to do with all this drug stuff. I—"

"You're here," Clarisse answered, "so that we can hear the truth."

"The truth?" Linc echoed.

"About what really happened that night after the party. You didn't go downstairs 'to pack up tiles,' did you? You didn't see Sweeney out of the apartment, did you? He died while you two were both up there, didn't he?"

"No," said Linc. "Honestly. He didn't."

"Us or the cops, Linc," said Valentine.

The noise from outside was growing louder and more raucous as midnight grew closer.

"All right," Linc said with resignation. "No, I didn't go downstairs. After we did it, he—"

Ashes seated himself on the edge of the desk next to Valentine to listen.

"—he went to the bathroom to wash up. I was in the living room and I heard this noise—it was like a firecracker. I thought he'd broken something, so I went down the hall to the bathroom. The door was closed, so I knocked, and when he didn't answer, I went in. He was lying on the floor and at first I thought he'd fainted. But when I turned him over I saw the bullet wound and the blood."

Linc was looking down at his hands. He raised his eyes. "Somebody shot him through the bathroom window." He glanced at Clarisse. "It was open about halfway and, since the sink is right next to the window, he must have been looking at himself in the mirror. Somebody out on the fire escape just reached inside and pulled the trigger, and that's all there was to it."

"What did you do?" Clarisse asked evenly.

"I took a towel out of the hamper, wrapped it around his head, and carried him into the bedroom and laid him out on the bed. Then I took the towel off him and went back to the bathroom and wiped up the blood. I put the towel in the dumpster behind District D."

"Didn't it occur to you to call the police?" Valentine inquired. "I mean, since Sweeney was shot and there wasn't a gun around, it would seem unlikely that you had done it."

"They would have thought I threw the gun away, and I was in an apartment that wasn't mine—and I had moved the body and everything."

"Why *did* you move the body?" asked Ashes curiously.

"I don't know," said Linc confusedly. "I don't know what I was thinking."

"Are you telling us the truth?" demanded Clarisse. "Or are you just getting a little nearer to it than you were before?"

Linc leveled his eyes on her. "It *is* the truth," he said with what seemed to be sincerity.

Valentine turned to his bar manager. "A stupid risk, Ashes," he said, "climbing the fire escape to shoot Sweeney."

Ashes seemed to have expected this. "I didn't do it," he said simply and calmly. "*I've* been telling the truth all along," he said, glancing at Linc.

"I think we'd better talk to Joe," said Clarisse, stepping toward the door. But the door was already opening of its own accord.

Outside, in the bar, the countdown had begun, at full volume. Every drunken man there was screaming the numbers.

TEN . . . NINE . . .

"Oh, God," said Valentine. "It's midnight."

The door opened all the way to reveal Miss America standing hesitantly on the threshold. Her mouth formed the words *Excuse me*, but nobody could actually hear her.

EIGHT . . . SEVEN . . . SIX . . .

"Not now, America!" shouted Clarisse.

FIVE . . . FOUR . . .

Clarisse started for the door, but before she could get to it, Miss America stepped inside the office and shut the door behind her. She smiled and opened her clutch bag. "Yes, now . . ." she said.

THREE . . . TWO . . .

Out of her bag, Miss America took a small .38-caliber pistol.

"It has to be now."

ONE.

Miss America began firing exactly as a deafening roar rose from the barroom below. Five hundred revelers were shouting at the tops of their lungs.

A bullet grazed Clarisse's shoulder, spattering blood across the white camellias. She dived behind the chair in which Linc was sitting.

Linc sprang for the desk.

Ashes raised a hand to his face and turned his head sideways. When a bullet ripped through the center of his palm, he shrieked and dropped to his knees.

Valentine leaped from his chair, but tripped, and fell back into it. The chair flipped over backward, and Valentine's head cracked loudly against the floorboards.

The third bullet Miss America fired hit the one-way mirror, and it shattered with a spectacular noise in a shower of glass. "Auld Lang Syne" and frantic cheering blasted into the room through the broken window. Black and white balloons and a storm of glitter were raining down upon the bar patrons. Just as Miss America aimed the gun at Clarisse's head and began to squeeze the trigger, the door behind her was flung open. The knob caught Miss America in the square of the back and she pitched forward. The gun fired into the floor very near Linc's foot as America's head slammed into the corner of the desk. A moment later Miss America slumped unconscious onto the carpet.

Joe stood framed in the doorway, one hand still on the knob.

"Oh, God, I'm sorry, Miss America," he said automatically, and then looked about in confusion at the mayhem.

Epilogue

"IT didn't happen," Mr. Fred moaned. *"Tell me it didn't happen."*
Clarisse touched the bandaged place on her left shoulder and and sighed, "I wish I *could* tell you that, Mr. Fred."

Valentine popped another Tab for Mr. Fred, and then poured more vodka into his and Clarisse's glasses.

It was four o'clock in the morning. Slate was a wreck. The last customers had staggered out just half an hour before. Felix and Larry had trudged home for a few hours' sleep before returning mid-morning to begin cleaning up. The floor of the bar was blanketed with confetti and the black and white skins of exploded balloons and was laced over with trampled streamers. Some balloons and streamers were still lodged here and there across the ceiling. Broken plastic champagne glasses were scattered on every flat surface available, and the bar was crowded with empty drink glasses and bottles of beer. Valentine had lowered the lights so that the debris was only a dim confusion, and they had dispensed with the tape. Music somehow didn't seem appropriate.

None of the bar patrons had been aware of the fracas in Valentine's office. Many people had seen the window of the office explode outward, exactly at midnight, but that accident had been ascribed to faulty renovation; fortunately, no one had been standing directly underneath. Valentine had summoned the police from across the street and taken them into the office through the interior entrance of the building. Clarisse, Ashes, and a groggy Miss America were taken to the emergency room of Boston City Hospital. Ashes was admitted for the night, while Clarisse was released once her flesh wound was cleaned and bandaged. Miss America, remanded into the custody of the police, confessed to the murder of Sweeney Drysdale II. She was charged and booked in night court. With a throbbing head, Valentine had been allowed to return to the bar and, assisted by Joe, had continued to serve his customers and to assure them that nothing was the matter.

When Clarisse got home, she changed from her blood-spattered gown into jeans and a loose long-sleeved blouse that hid her bandage. She wandered back down to the bar as Joe and Valentine were pushing out the diehards.

A few minutes later Mr. Fred, still in his red-sequined jacket, beat at the locked front doors. He was returning from his sister's arraignment, and was desperate to find out what had happened to turn his whole world upside down. Clarisse had taken him into the kitchen of the bar and told him everything she knew of the business—what she had found out indirectly, what she had heard across the street, what she now surmised. When everyone was gone, Clarisse had led Mr. Fred out to the bar and Valentine had set him up with the first of many Tabs.

Although he'd only had soda to drink all night, Mr. Fred seemed more than a little drunk now. Clarisse charitably ascribed this to his remorse over his sister's predicament.

"Oh, God," groaned Fred. "America in jail! Accused of murder! She's sitting in a cell down at Charles Street with a Band-Aid on her head!" He took a breath and looked at Valentine and Clarisse.

"She was trying to protect you," Valentine pointed out. "Though she didn't go about it in a very intelligent fashion."

"A reporter took our picture!" Mr. Fred moaned. "It'll prob- ably end up on the front page of the *Herald*–MISS AMERICA ON .38-CALIBER SPREE. Ma's gonna have a heart attack. Rosaries and holy water'll be flying all over the North End." He stifled another moan with a swig of Tab. "And what'll happen after they get done investigating? They'll find out about Ashes and me. I'll spend the rest of my life in Walpole. I'll end up a hairdresser to the unparoled! Oh, God!!"

Neither Valentine nor Clarisse said anything. Both put their glasses of vodka to their lips and drank deeply.

"Where did America get the gun, Fred?" asked Valentine.

"I didn't even know she had it!" he cried. "Guns make me ner- vous. She told the police she got it through a mail order ad in one of those outdoor magazines she's always reading."

"So it wasn't registered?"

"I don't think so," said Mr. Fred.

"Why did she get it in the first place?" Valentine asked.

"She said it was to protect herself from the bears in Yellowstone," said Mr. Fred.

"It's a lucky thing she didn't take target practice," remarked Clarisse. "I never saw anybody with such a bad aim. The only reason she was able to kill Sweeney was that she put the gun right up to his temple. That *was* America up on the roof with the Betamax, wasn't it?"

"She confessed to that, too," sighed Mr. Fred.

"Where did she get it?" Valentine asked. "You didn't have one, did you?"

"No, but I had bought that one for her birthday. It was going to be a surprise, and I had hidden it in the back room of the shop. I guess I didn't hide it well enough. I thought it was still back there."

"Do you have a lawyer?" Valentine asked.

Fred nodded. "I called him from the police station. He's already over at the jail. I think he's going to try to have the charge reduced to manslaughter."

"Manslaughter!" sputtered Clarisse. "She climbed four stories up a fire escape at night and blew away your ex-lover at point-blank range! She stood on the roof of the building next door and hurled a video cassette recorder at my head! She carried a loaded gun in her clutch bag and sprayed a room with bullets! And your lawyer wants to call it *manslaughter?*"

Mr. Fred blinked. "She was confused," he said complacently.

Valentine and Clarisse glanced at one another. Clarisse closed her eyes and shook her head.

"Mr. Fred," said Valentine, "I think it's time for you to go home. I'm going to call you a taxi."

Mr. Fred nodded. "Can I take a couple of Tabs with me?"

Valentine got a six-pack out of a cooler, then punched out a number on the telephone and ordered a cab. A few minutes later it was out front, blowing its horn. Valentine and Clarisse saw Mr. Fred to the door. A light snow had begun to fall, and the street was glazed with a dusting of white.

Mr. Fred waved sadly at them as he climbed in the back of the cab with the six-pack.

———

———

"LET'S go for a walk," said Clarisse, looking up and down the almost deserted street.

"All right," said Valentine. He went back inside and returned with two leather bomber jackets. He handed the smaller to Clarisse, explaining, "Left in the coat check." Clarisse struggled into hers and Valentine locked the doors of the bar. Clarisse tucked her hands into the pockets of the jacket for warmth; a moment later she withdrew a pack of Marlboros from the left-hand pocket. She and Valentine looked at the pack, and then at each other. Clarisse crumpled the pack in her fist and tossed it into a trash basket attached to a lamppost. They took off slowly down the middle of Warren Avenue, arm-in-arm.

"There's something I still don't understand," said Clarisse. "How did America know that Sweeney and Linc were up in my apartment?"

"She was probably at the front of the shop and looked out the window and saw Sweeney and Linc go into our building. So she went out the back way and climbed up the fire escape, looking in all the windows on the way up. Finally she saw them in your apartment—if you look through your bedroom window you can see all the way to the living room. She probably waited to see if Sweeney would come into the bedroom—or the bathroom. And when he did, she shot him. Then she just went back down the fire escape and rejoined the party. Nobody noticed she'd been missing."

"I feel sorry for Fred. He's the one who's lost everything. It wasn't his fault that America was so possessive and protective. Of course, he shouldn't have been selling drugs."

"And Ashes ought not to have been supplying him," added Valentine. "I'm not sure what I'm going to do about that."

"Do you think the media will play this up? I'm not so sure I want my name and photograph all over the front page this time."

"I don't want to think about it tonight. I just want to crash until Easter."

"Slate is opening again at three o'clock tomorrow afternoon," Clarisse pointed out. "*This* afternoon. A full buffet."

"You'll help out with it, won't you?"

"I will be useful as well as ornamental. And speaking of use and ornament, what happened to Linc? I lost sight of him."

"He was upset—being shot at. So he got drunker than he already was. And then when we brought the lights up, he went home with the first three men he could find that could still walk. Linc will be fine. I'm not worried about him."

They said nothing for another block.

"How's your arm?" Valentine asked.

"I'll have an interesting scar at poolside. How's the bump on your head?"